# The Wonderf

c

# Uncle

by
## Richard Anderson

*To Bradley*

illustrated by
## Stewart Anderson

*Richard Anderson*

# www.unclewizard.co.uk

**RR**

**Rules Review Publishing Limited**
London

The Wonderful Adventure of Uncle Wizard

Published by Rules Review Publishing Ltd.
78 Brookdene Road, London, SE18 1EJ

www.rulesreview.co.uk

First published 2009

1

ISBN 978-0-9563836-0-0

Printed and bound in Great Britain by TJ International Ltd, Padstow, Cornwall

For mum and dad

# 1

Uncle Wizard lived in a wigwam at the end of Happy Apple Lane. He had big kind eyes, a cheery smile and was quite possibly the worst wizard in the world.

'Wait a minute, that's not right…'

Uncle Wizard stared at the spell he was mixing inside his magic pot. Instead of being green and bubbling, it was purple and on fire.

'Oh well,' he said with a shrug, 'perhaps it just needs a dash of whiz-bang powder, here goes…'

*KABOOM!*

'Aaaaarrrgghhh!'

There was an ear-splitting explosion. Uncle Wizard was lifted clean off his feet and hurled right across the wigwam. He landed in a tangled heap underneath the kitchen table.

'Crumbs!' he said, climbing groggily to his feet, 'that was a lively one! Well Bob, did it work? Was my spell a success?'

Over on his perch Bob the Pigeon looked up from the magazine he was reading and shook his head.

'I wouldn't exactly call it a success.'

Uncle Wizard frowned.

'Why, what would you call it, then?'

'Well, the word *disaster* springs to mind,' said Bob. 'I mean, you were trying to turn a saucepan into an umbrella, when what you've actually done is turn the fridge into a penguin...'

Over in the kitchen a rather bemused looking

penguin stared at Uncle Wizard. It then frowned, ruffled its feathers and plodded out of the wigwam and off down Happy Apple Lane.

'...no wonder you're banned from the MagicMania 8 celebrations.'

'Now, now, Bob, I may not be one of the Great Wizards and occasionally there may be slight errors with my spells, but...'

Bob shook his head again. He had heard Uncle Wizard's excuses a thousand times and went back to reading his *Pigeon World* magazine. He was particularly interested in an article on pies. Bob loved pies. In fact Bob loved pies so much he visited Mr Wobble's Pie Shop three times a day.

'...anyway,' continued Uncle Wizard, 'just because I'm banned from MagicMania 8, doesn't mean I'm hopeless at spells.'

Bob threw up his wings in disbelief.

'Yes it does!' he exclaimed, 'you sucked all the clouds out of the sky with that enchanted vacuum cleaner spell. It took the Great Wizards a whole month to put them all back again.'

Uncle Wizard grimaced.

'Well, it's not easy when this is the only spell book I've got. Half the pages are missing and the last five chapters are about smells not spells. I'd probably be better off without it...'

Suddenly his face lit up.

'...wait a minute, that's it! It must be the spell book's fault. I'd do better if I just made the spells up myself...'

Bob looked aghast.

'I'm not sure that's such a good idea...'

But Uncle Wizard had already started mixing his next spell. Into his magic pot went plunder-gas and boom-powder. There was a slug of slog-juice, three boing-boing rocks and a wisp of moon-smoke. Within seconds the whole wigwam wailed and shook like a hyper-goblin disco.

'And now,' cried Uncle Wizard with eager eyes, 'a double dose of whiz-bang powder!'

Uncle Wizard measured out the whiz-bang powder and held it over the spell. He began to pour, paused, smiled a gleeful smile, and then tossed the whole bottle of whiz-bang powder into the spell.

*KABOOOOOOOOOOOOM!*

'Aaaaarrrgghhh!'

There was a thunderous explosion! Uncle Wizard blasted out of the wigwam as if he were a space-rocket. His feet were on fire and smoke poured out of his ears. Over and over he went, turning cartwheels and somersaults, tumbling through the sky like a rag-doll. He wailed and screamed, cried for help, before crash-landing upside down in a pear tree. The branches creaked, groaned and then suddenly snapped. Uncle Wizard hit the floor with a painful thud.

'Why me?' he cried in despair. 'What have I ever done wrong? I might never be Wizard of the Year, but surely, just once, I could make a spell that worked?'

At that moment a juicy pear fell from the tree and landed with a splat on Uncle Wizard's head.

'Why do I bother? I might as well give up being a wizard. What's the point of magic?'

The afternoon drifted slowly by. Uncle Wizard sat under the pear tree with his head in his hands. He was finished with being a wizard. He would burn his magic hat, throw away his potions and powders and cancel his subscription to Magic Monthly.

In utter despair he stumbled across the field towards a grimy pond. The water was dark and deep. He took out his spell book and held it above his head, ready to hurl it into the pond.

'I'm the worst wizard in the world, truly I am.'

Just then, from the far side of the field, came a desperate cry. Uncle Wizard looked over and saw a strange creature hurtling across the grass. The creature cried out again. It was a frantic, terrified cry. Uncle Wizard was shocked. It was Bob the Pigeon.

'Good grief!' said Uncle Wizard in amazement.

Bob bounded across the grass with a look of utter panic on his face. Uncle Wizard ran to meet him.

'There you are, there you are,' said Bob wheezing and coughing. 'I've been looking everywhere for you.'

'What is it?' asked Uncle Wizard worriedly, 'what's happened?'

Bob took a moment to recover his breath.

'It's terrible!' he panted. 'Just terrible! Uncle Wizard, only you can save the world!'

# 2

Uncle Wizard burst into the wigwam. A few seconds later Bob staggered in and pointed breathlessly at the television.

'Look! Look!'

On the screen was Enchantment Castle. It was decked with sparkling lights to celebrate MagicMania 8. But the lights were pale and lifeless. Dark clouds filled the sky. At a safe distance from the castle a television reporter spoke rapidly into a microphone.

*'...today was supposed to be a day of joy. All the Great Wizards, all the wizards from around the world here on Illusion Island for the MagicMania 8 celebrations...but now it is a day of disaster...'*

Suddenly the drawbridge of Enchantment Castle began to lower. It creaked and groaned, then thudded into place across the moat. From the courtyard came the sound of laughter. It was a grotesque, evil laugh.

The reporter cried out in terror.

*'…we're all doomed, HE has escaped…'*

Lightning crashed across the sky. Rain pelted down. Across the drawbridge strode a figure dressed in a cloak of nightmare darkness.

*'I AM GRIM WIZARD...'*

Grim Wizard threw up his arms. Devil-light sparked on his bony fingers. He uttered the words of a hideous spell and two flaming fire-balls blasted towards the screaming crowd. They smashed into the road and sent wreckage hurtling in every direction.

*'…I HAVE ESCAPED.'*

His eyes glowed like raging volcanoes. His skin was covered with seeping boils. He raised his head to the sky and roared with fury.

*'I HAVE DEFEATED THE GREAT WIZARDS. I HAVE BANISHED THEM TO ANOTHER LAND. ENCHANTMENT CASTLE IS MINE. NOW I SHALL CAPTURE WIZARD HQ AND RULE THE WORLD!'*

The news-reporter shook with fear.

*'…Grim Wizard has escaped. He has defeated the Great Wizards. If there's any wizard out there, any wizard at all, you must go to Wizard HQ. You must get there before Grim Wizard arrives. You must save us all…'*

Uncle Wizard turned off the television.

'Its me,' he said quietly, 'I'm the only wizard left. Only I can save the world.'

Uncle Wizard slumped on the sofa and stared blankly into space. How could he possibly defeat Grim Wizard? Grim Wizard was the most evil wizard to ever live. He had defeated the Great Wizards and banished them to another land. What chance did he have?

Bob shivered. Grim Wizard's voice had sent a chill running down his spine. He looked up at Uncle Wizard hopefully.

'You can do it, can't you?' he asked nervously. 'You can save the world?'

Uncle Wizard sighed. It was hopeless. No one could defeat Grim Wizard, certainly not him. He turned round to Bob, ready to shake his head. And then he saw the look in Bob's eyes. Bob was terrified. The whole world was doomed. Suddenly Uncle Wizard realised. He must save the world. Everyone was counting on him. Not just Bob, not just the Great Wizards, but everyone.

'Can I do it?'

Bob nodded.

'Yes, can you save the world?'

For a moment Uncle Wizard was silent. The fate of the world rested on this moment. Suddenly an enormous grin burst out on his face.

'Of course I can save the world...I'm Uncle Wizard!'

Bob sighed with relief.

'Well, good luck then, let me know how you get on.'

'Oh no,' said Uncle Wizard, shaking his head, 'if I'm saving the world, you're coming with me.'

Bob looked utterly terrified.

'But…but…but…' he spluttered, desperately thinking of an excuse 'I can't save the world, I'm needed here. Who's going to eat all the pies in Mr Wobble's Pie Shop?'

'I think you've eaten enough pies recently,' said Uncle Wizard. 'The exercise will do you good!'

'Excuse me!' exclaimed Bob. 'Are you saying I'm a fat pigeon? I'll have you know I'm the most athletic pigeon in the whole of Happy Apple Lane.'

Uncle Wizard groaned.

'Athletic! You can't even fly! We leave for Wizard HQ in five minutes. Get packing!'

Uncle Wizard grabbed his spell book and his powders and potions. He unplugged the television, made sure his enchanted vacuum cleaner was safely locked away, and left a note for the milkman (the note said, *sorry for turning you into a turnip*).

'Ready then, Bob?'

Bob frowned.

'Do I really have to come?'

'Not if you don't want to...'

Bob sighed with relief.

'…but I'm taking all the pies with me.'

In a flash Bob put on his bobble hat, knotted his scarf and stood by the wigwam's door.

Uncle Wizard smiled.

'Excellent! All set?'

'Lets do it.'

And with that Uncle Wizard and Bob the Pigeon left the wigwam and set off to save the world.

# 3

The sky above the big city was dark and ominous. A chill wind blew and rain drizzled down. Uncle Wizard wrapped his wizard's cloak tightly around his body and Bob adjusted his scarf.

'Come on,' said Uncle Wizard, 'we've got to get to Wizard HQ before Grim Wizard arrives.'

They hurried along Potion Parade and into Mystical Boulevard. At the House of Conjurors they turned left, passed by the statue of the Wise Witches and then turned left again into Magic Avenue. Up ahead, eerily silent and wrapped in a blanket of swirling fog lay the entrance to Wizard Street.

Bob tugged at his bobble hat nervously.

'I don't like the look of this.'

Uncle Wizard grimaced.

'I've never seen it like this before. Normally Wizard Street is fizzing with magic. It just looks…lifeless.'

'You don't think Grim Wizard is here already?'

Uncle Wizard peered nervously down Wizard Street. The fog was so thick even Wizard HQ was hidden from view.

'Well, there's only one way to find out…'

Uncle Wizard took a deep breath, stepped into Wizard Street, and immediately disappeared in the swirling fog. Bob took an anxious look around and then quickly followed after him.

'I can't see a thing. Where are you?'

'I'm over here,' called Uncle Wizard.

'Where's here?' asked Bob.

Uncle Wizard paused uncertainly.

'Erm…I'm not sure.'

They managed to find each other by the pale glow of a lamppost and edged slowly forwards. Bob was terrified. In the fog every street light looked like the eye of a mega-demon, and every howl of the wind sounded like the cry of an ooze-goblin. He felt certain something was going to leap out and eat him.

'Where's Wizard HQ?' he asked desperately.

Uncle Wizard shrugged.

'Its at the end of the street. We should be able to see it by now.'

Suddenly, out of the fog a face appeared.

'Aaaaarrrggghhh!' cried Bob, 'It's Grim Wizard, we're done for!'

Uncle Wizard gasped and dived into his pocket for his spell book. He desperately flicked through the pages looking for a *running away* spell, but then let out a huge sigh of relief.

'No, no, that's not Grim Wizard. That's a statue of King Wizard. It's Wizard HQ! We've arrived!'

They dashed forward and the whole of Wizard HQ suddenly appeared. Even in its darkest hour it was still a breathtaking sight.

Wizard HQ was built of spells. One incredible spell after another laid the foundations and the building grew in every which way it pleased. It stretched high into the sky and disappeared deep underground. There were statues of the Great Wizards and carvings of fantastical beings with three heads and spinning eyes. At the very top of Wizard HQ sat a huge chimney. When Wizard HQ bustled with life the chimney would spurt out great bursts of magic into the sky above. The clouds would sparkle with the most incredible colours. But today, like the rest of Wizard HQ, it was cold and lifeless.

Uncle Wizard shivered.

'Come on, we better get inside.'

They quickly climbed the marble steps and stood before the Great Oak Door of Wizard HQ.

'Now,' said Uncle Wizard, 'I'll just ring the bell…'

He pulled on a golden rope and a huge bell chimed inside Wizard HQ. For a moment there was silence, then came the sound of footsteps from within. They grew louder and louder before coming to a halt on the other side of the Great Oak Door. A key entered the lock.

Suddenly Bob had a thought.

'Erm, if all the wizards have been captured, who's actually opening the door?'

Uncle Wizard froze. A look of horror appeared on his face.

'Grim Wizard!'

Uncle Wizard and Bob stared at the door. It clicked, groaned and then sprung open with terrifying speed. Two hands emerged from within. They were old and wrinkled. With looks of horror on their faces Uncle Wizard and Bob turned to flee, but it was too late. The hands reached out, grabbed their collars and yanked them into the darkness of Wizard HQ.

'Aarrgh!' screamed Uncle Wizard.

'Aaaaarrrggghhh!' screamed Bob the Pigeon.

# 4

Uncle Wizard and Bob landed in a heap in the lobby of Wizard HQ. They desperately tried to struggle to their feet, but two powerful hands pinned them to the floor. With a heart-wrenching sound the Great Oak Door slammed shut.

'Let go of us!' exclaimed Bob.

'You wont get away with this!' cried Uncle Wizard.

'Will you two please be quiet!' said an impatient voice. 'Grim Wizard could be here at any moment…'

'Huh?' spluttered Uncle Wizard, utterly confused.

'And what were you doing coming in the main entrance? Grim Wizard will know you're here now. You're the only wizard left, by thunder! You've got to be more careful.'

With a yank Uncle Wizard and Bob were pulled to their feet. It took a moment for their eyes to adjust to the darkness before a look of utter relief came over their faces.

'Harris the Caretaker!' exclaimed Uncle Wizard with joy.

Stood before them was a gruff old man. He wore a battered coat, a tatty cap and shabby shoes. Harris was the caretaker of Wizard HQ. No one knew the twisting, turning labyrinths of Wizard HQ better than Harris the Caretaker.

'At your service,' said Harris tipping his cap.

'But we must hurry, that door wont hold Grim Wizard when he gets here.'

Harris led them across the Grand Lobby of Wizard HQ. They raced down the Corridor of Mystery and charged through the Hall of Spells. A winding passageway led them to the Amulet Staircase, and then onto the Chamber of the Ancient Wizards. Finally they stopped outside a plain looking door. With a serious look on his face Harris turned to Uncle Wizard.

'We haven't much time. Grim Wizard must be stopped or the world is doomed. Uncle Wizard, you are the only wizard left. You must defeat Grim Wizard.'

Uncle Wizard tugged at his collar nervously.

'How can I possibly defeat Grim Wizard?'

'With a spell,' said Harris.

'What spell?'

Harris smiled.

'One of these might help…'

With a dramatic flourish Harris the Caretaker threw open the door. There was a flash of colour and a sparkle of light. Before them lay the most extraordinary room in the whole of Wizard HQ.

'The Secret Library,' gasped Uncle Wizard in amazement. 'We're in The Secret Library!'

There were spell books everywhere, millions of them. Some sat on bookcases that stretched to the ceiling. Others glowed with eerie moonlight. Some even had wings and flew about The Secret Library like birds.

'It's incredible,' said Uncle Wizard.

Harris smiled.

'It certainly is. You can always find me in The Secret Library, should you need to. But quickly, this way.'

Harris led them along an aisle of towering bookcases and past a shelf of spell books with blinking eyes. They crossed the dusty floor until a small flight of stairs took them down into the darkest, most cobweb ridden corner of The Secret Library.

'There is only one spell that can defeat Grim Wizard,' said Harris, 'but it wont be easy…'

Tucked away on a forgotten shelf lay an ancient casket. Harris pulled out a key and the casket opened with a yawning creak. Inside was a scroll. It was yellow and dry and its edges flaked at the slightest touch. Harris passed it to Uncle

Wizard.

'This is the Spell of Forever.'

Uncle Wizard took the scroll and unrolled it carefully. He studied it for a moment, then with a puzzled expression turned it over and studied the other side.

'Erm…there's not actually anything written on it?'

Harris nodded.

'The Spell of Forever is such an important spell, the words are hidden away…'

'Right,' said Uncle Wizard uncertainly, 'so where do I find the words?'

Harris took a deep breath.

'The Witch has them.'

'The Witch?' said Uncle Wizard disbelievingly. 'But there's no such thing as witches anymore.'

Harris smiled.

'You've got a lot to learn. Now, come on…'

As Harris spoke the whole of Wizard HQ suddenly shook. Dust splattered down from the ceiling and spell books crashed to the floor. On the far side of The Secret Library the air suddenly grew black and poisonous. A violent wind whipped through the library and hideous laughter filled the room. From out of the darkness appeared a terrifying figure.

'Grim Wizard is here!' cried Bob in alarm.

In his cloak of nightmare darkness, Grim Wizard stood like a giant in The Secret Library. He took one pace forward and stared down upon Uncle Wizard.

'WHO ARE YOU?'

Uncle Wizard gulped.  He tried to speak, but his throat was dry.

'ANSWER ME!'

With a deep breath he looked up at Grim Wizard.

'My name is Uncle Wizard.  I am here to save the world.'

Grim Wizard laughed.  It was a dreadful, heartless sound.

'YOU WILL SAVE NOTHING, PATHETIC WIZARD.'

Grim Wizard's eyes raged with fire.  He raised his arms and devil-light blasted across The Secret

Library.

'Hold tight!' cried Harris the Caretaker.

'What?' screamed Uncle Wizard.

Harris grabbed hold of Uncle Wizard and Bob as the devil-light flashed across the room.   He yanked a lever on the wall and suddenly a trap door opened beneath them.  They fell like stones through the hole in the floor.

'Aargh!' screamed Uncle Wizard.

'Aaaaaarrrgghhh!' screamed Bob the Pigeon.

With a thud they landed on the floor in the corridor beneath the Secret Library.

'Come on,' said Harris, 'Grim Wizard wont be far behind.  We must hurry.'

'Where are we going?' asked Bob.

'To a place of wonder and joy,' said Harris.

'Mr Wobble's pie shop?' asked Bob hopefully.

'To find The Witch!' said Harris.  'Now hurry!'

Harris grabbed an oil-burning lamp from the wall and they raced into the underground realms of Wizard HQ.  The deeper they went the darker it became.  The corridors flickered with shadows and cobwebs caught in their hair.  They leapt down spiralling staircases and slid down slippery chutes. Deeper and deeper they went until the floor was thick with mud.  Slime oozed from the walls and bug-eyed creatures scuttled about on hairy legs.

Suddenly the corridor exploded with devil-light.

'YOU CANNOT ESCAPE ME, PATHETIC WIZARD.'

Grim Wizard was behind them.  His cloak of nightmare darkness flapped in the cold air and his red eyes burnt through the darkness.

Harris urged them on.

'Keeping running. You must find The Witch.'

Down and down Harris took them. They dashed along corridors, leapt down staircases, but with every step Grim Wizard gained on them. Finally they came to a passageway at the very bottom of Wizard HQ. The floor squelched. The walls were alive with wriggling bugs.

'This is as far as I go,' said Harris.

'What about us?' asked Bob.

Harris held the oil-burning torch out in front of him and lit up the passageway. At the far end stood a single, brilliant white door.

'You must go through that door.'

'Where does it lead?'

'It leads to the Land of Forever. A land bursting with so much magic you'll wont believe your eyes. There you will find The Witch.'

'But what about you?' asked Uncle Wizard.

'Just go!'

Uncle Wizard and Bob splashed through the mud and raced towards the gleaming white door. As they reached it a thunderous roar echoed through the passageway. Uncle Wizard turned and there in the darkness glowed Grim Wizard's evil red eyes.

'I WILL DESTROY YOU PATHETIC WIZARD!'

'Go now!' cried Harris.

The door was old and heavy. As Uncle Wizard grabbed the handle Grim Wizard barged past Harris and thundered towards them.

'Open the door!,' screamed Bob.

Uncle Wizard turned the handle, but it was stuck fast.

'YOU WILL NOT ESCAPE THIS TIME.'

Grim Wizard closed in. Devil-light sparked on his fingers. With a raging cry he raised his arms.

'Pull harder!' cried Bob.

'It wont budge!'

Uncle Wizard pulled and pulled. Every muscle in his body strained and his face turned red. Suddenly there was a click. The handle turned, the hinges creaked and the door budged open an inch.

'AND NOW PATHETIC WIZARD, YOU WILL BE DESTROYED…'

Desperately Uncle Wizard pulled harder. The door opened another inch, then another. The gap grew bigger. A blast of devil-light crashed above their heads.

'Now Bob, now!'

The gap was big enough. Without a thought Uncle Wizard and Bob dived through to the other side. Slowly, creakingly the door began to close.

Grim Wizard lunged for the closing door. His bony fingers clawed at the gap. They scraped and scratched but the door clicked shut.

'OPEN THIS DOOR.'

'That door will never open for you,' said Harris.

Suddenly Grim Wizard turned around. His face boiled with rage.

'I COMMAND YOU…'

But Harris had vanished into the shadows. The passageway was empty.

Grim Wizard banged on the door with utter fury.

'I WILL FIND YOU, PATHETIC WIZARD. I WILL FIND YOU AND DESTROY YOU!'

# 5

Uncle Wizard and Bob tumbled like dice into the Land of Forever. They collapsed in a breathless heap and stared at the sky.

'Good grief!' said Uncle Wizard.

'Crumbs!' said Bob.

High in the sky, blazing brightly, were two giant suns. One was yellow, the other was red and they bathed the land in sumptuous colour. Uncle Wizard struggled to his feet and rubbed his eyes in amazement.

'I've never seen anything like it.'

'Marvellous, isn't it?' said a passing tree.

Uncle Wizard was agog. An enormous tree with pea-green leaves walked casually past them as if it were the most natural thing in the world. Bob tugged at his bobble hat nervously.

'I hope this is the Land of Forever, otherwise we've both gone quite, quite mad.'

They found themselves in a gloriously green field surrounded by the most idyllic countryside. Uncle Wizard turned around and there, in the middle of the field, stood the brilliant white door which led back to Wizard HQ.

'Did we really come through that?' asked Bob.

Uncle Wizard nodded. For a moment he thought about the evil red eyes of Grim Wizard and his growling, hideous voice.

'Come on, we don't want to wait around for Grim Wizard to catch us. Lets go and find The

Witch.'

They set off across the field. The Land of Forever was full of wonders. A rainbow-stream trickled into the valley below, and upon a lily-pad a bubble-frog sat chatting to a mega-toad. High in the sky a flock of rocket-bats swooped and soared on the swirling breeze. At the edge of the field a path wound its way through the valley and up over a hill. With the suns beating on their backs, Uncle Wizard and Bob set off towards the hill.

'Well, this is most agreeable,' said Uncle Wizard.

Bob nodded.

'We should save the world more often.'

The path was dotted with sparkle-flowers and glitter-bushes. A family of humming-bunnies popped out from a hole in the ground. As Uncle Wizard and Bob walked by they hummed a tune so beautiful the whole land seemed to sigh in contentment.

The path meandered past a meadow of whistle-grass before finally reaching the foot of the hill. Uncle Wizard and Bob puffed their way to the summit and with rosy cheeks paused to admire the wondrous view below.

'Wow!' said Bob in amazement.

Far to the east lay the Algebra-Forest where the abacus-tree grew in great numbers. Dominating the west were the Boom-Mountains, home of the waddling-rocks. From the south came the lowly moan of the Sulking Sea and from the north came the sizzle and roar of the Molten Waterfalls.

'Good day, sirs!'

Uncle Wizard looked to the sky and there, soaring and swooping with amazing grace were two flying-cows.

'Err, hello,' replied Uncle Wizard uncertainly.

The two flying-cows performed an elaborate loop-the-loop before landing with a twinkle of feet in front of Uncle Wizard and Bob.

'I am Lance,' said the first flying-cow with a theatrical bow.

'And I am Stallion,' said the second.

Uncle Wizard introduced himself and Bob.

'Beautiful day,' he said.

Lance the Flying-Cow raised his eyebrows and stared dismissively at Uncle Wizard.

'Is it? Yes, I suppose it is,' he said haughtily,

'though not as beautiful as Stallion and I.'

'I'm sorry?' said Uncle Wizard.

'Oh yes,' said Stallion, 'we flying-cows are simply quite beautiful, the most beautiful creatures in the whole of the Land of Forever. More beautiful than anything…especially *her*.'

Uncle Wizard raised his eyebrows.

'*Her*?'

Stallion shook his head abruptly.

'Do not bother yourself with *her*. There are some foolish people in the Land of Forever that say *she* is more beautiful than us flying-cows.'

'But she is quite, quite ugly,' added Lance.

'Who is?' asked Uncle Wizard.

'The Witch,' said the cows in unison.

Uncle Wizard's eyes lit up. The Witch, just who they were looking for.

'Can you take us to see her?' he asked hopefully.

Lance and Stallion looked astonished.

'Why would you want to see *her*? She is almost as ugly as that pigeon…'

'I beg your pardon!' cried Bob indignantly, 'I happen to be considered something of a catch in pigeon circles. Why, I was once romantically linked to Princess Pigeonetta…'

'Yes,' agreed Uncle Wizard with a sigh, 'right up until she threatened to have your head cut off. But anyway,' he continued, turning back to Lance and Stallion, 'it's very important that we find The Witch.'

The two flying-cows muttered to one another.

'Very well,' said Stallion reluctantly. 'We will take you to her cottage…'

'…but we wont look at her,' added Lance quickly.

Uncle Wizard beamed with pleasure and then he and Bob clambered aboard Lance. With one mighty beat of his wings Lance the flying-cow leapt into the air, and they were soon soaring amongst the clouds.

'Are you sure this is safe?' asked Bob nervously.

'Oh yes,' said Uncle Wizard calmly, 'the flying-cow has an excellent air-safety record.'

'Is that true?' asked Bob suspiciously.

'Well,' said Uncle Wizard, 'it's more of a guess, really, but…'

But Uncle Wizard never got to finish his sentence. With a mighty whoosh of his magnificent wings Lance performed a heart-stopping loop-the-loop.

'Woooooooooh!' cried Uncle Wizard.

'Aaaaarrrggghhh!' screamed Bob the Pigeon.

On and on they flew. The views were astonishing. There was a multicoloured beach and cliffs of sparkling gold. A giant sea-elephant burst out of the ocean and leapt clean above the waves. For a second it hung majestically in mid-air before splashing back down into the glistening waters.

They swooped over valleys and hills. They glided over forests and rivers. For a brief second they caught sight of a family of water-snakes. Huge long snakes made entirely of water slithering rapidly between the trunks of bongo-trees.

Suddenly, in the distance, Uncle Wizard spotted a plume of smoke rising into the air from a quaint little cottage. He tapped Bob on the shoulder.

'The cottage! That must be where The Witch lives.'

It was simply beautiful. The cottage was thatched with golden straw and song-birds chirped in the garden. The flying-cows swooped down and with a gentle bump they landed by the cottage. Uncle Wizard and Bob clambered onto the ground.

'What a positively revolting cottage,' said Lance sneeringly.

'It makes one feel quite ill,' agreed Stallion.

'Come, let us leave this place before we catch sight of her. She is so ugly she may turn us to stone.'

With a dramatic toss of their heads the flying-cows flapped their wings and soared off into the sky. For a moment Uncle Wizard and Bob watched them go, then turned to face the cottage.

'So,' said Bob, 'is this witch really as ugly as those cows said?'

Uncle Wizard shrugged his shoulders.

'I don't know. I've never seen a witch before. No wizard has, not for a hundred years...'

# 6

Uncle Wizard knocked on the door of the cottage and anxiously twiddled the tassels of his magic cloak. Dainty feet approached and with a gentle click the door opened.

'Crikes!' exclaimed Uncle Wizard.

The Witch was so beautiful Uncle Wizard almost yanked the tassels clean off his magic cloak. Her hair was golden, her eyes sparkled, and she had a smile that would light up a moonless night.

'Oh my,' said The Witch with surprise, 'a wizard! Well, well, I am honoured.'

Uncle Wizard bowed elaborately.

'Good day to you Madam Witch.'

'And good day to you Master Wizard, and also to you Mister Pigeon. Well, wont you two come inside for a cup of tea, I've just finished baking a pie…'

'Pie!' exclaimed Bob joyously. 'Did someone say *pie*? I definitely heard the word *pie*. Take me to the pie…'

With a smile The Witch led them inside. The cottage was as exquisite on the inside as it was on the outside. A roaring log-fire crackled in the living room, and a glorious aroma of fresh baking wafted in from the kitchen. Bob sat on the sofa and drooled like a puppy at the pie that was laid before him.

'Please,' said The Witch, 'dig in.'

Bob stared at the pie with ravenous eyes. He

licked his lips and dived straight in.

'You'll get fat,' said Uncle Wizard.

Bob paused, his mouth full of pie.

'That's a chance I'm willing to take.'

The Witch poured the tea and passed a cup to Uncle Wizard.

'So, then Master Wizard...'

'Please, call me Uncle Wizard.'

'So then Uncle Wizard, what brings you to the Land of Forever?'

Uncle Wizard shuffled uneasily in his seat and frowned. He then reached inside his magic cloak and pulled out the Spell of Forever.

'This does…'

The Witch gasped. Her face turned ghostly white.

'Oh my, *He* has returned...?'

'The Great Wizards have been captured,' said Uncle Wizard gravely. 'Grim Wizard now rules the world. I am the only wizard left.'

The living room fell silent. The Witch stared out of the window and shook her head sadly. A single tear trickled down her cheek. Painful memories from long ago flashed before her eyes.

'I have encountered Grim Wizard before,' she said slowly. 'Long ago the Wise Witches fought him, but we were no match for his terrible magic. One by one the witches disappeared, never to be seen again. You must not let the same fate befall the wizards. You must stop Grim Wizard.'

Uncle Wizard gulped. The more he heard about Grim Wizard, the more terrifying his situation became.

'Can he be defeated?'

'Only a wizard can defeat Grim Wizard,' said The Witch, 'and only by using the Spell of Forever.'

Uncle Wizard stared at the scroll. As it had been in the Great Library the scroll was blank on both sides.

'But there's nothing written on it...'

The Witch nodded.

'The Spell of Forever is astonishingly powerful. Long ago the Great Wizards asked me to keep the words of the spell hidden away. They hoped it would never come to this, but now it is time to return the spell…'

The room became eerily silent. The Witch whispered the words of an enchanted spell and her fingers glowed with magical-fizzing sparkles. Everything shone with a starry brilliance. It was the purest, most wondrous magic Uncle Wizard had ever seen.

'Hold tight,' said The Witch.

The room came alive. Like electric-bees the magical-fizzing sparkles leapt into the air and swarmed around the room. There was a kaleidoscope of colour. Suddenly the sparkles dived towards the Spell of Forever. One after another they thudded onto the scroll. Uncle Wizard could barely believe his eyes. As the sparkles landed they turned into letters. The letters then turned into words. Before Uncle Wizard's eyes was the most incredible spell he had ever seen.

'I…I don't understand.'

'The Spell of Forever has three parts,' said The Witch. 'You must find each part before you can defeat Grim Wizard.'

'But, I can't read any of the three parts.'

'The Spell of Forever is a secret spell. You can only read the third part of the spell once you have found the second part, and the second part only when you have found the first.'

'But I can't even read the first part…!'

*ORT LLURN ED T HAFOHOT TOHTE*

The Witch clicked her fingers. Slowly the letters of the first part of the spell began to rearrange themselves on the scroll. They bumped and jostled across the paper until suddenly, with a flash of brilliant light, the first part of the spell was revealed. Uncle Wizard re-read the Spell of Forever. His mouth dropped open in astonishment.

'What is it?' asked Bob, wiping crumbs of pie from his mouth, 'what's the first thing we need to find?'

Uncle Wizard showed Bob the spell.

## *THE TOOTH OF A THUNDER TROLL*

'Aah,' said Uncle Wizard.
'Oh dear,' said Bob the Pigeon.

# 7

'Now, have you got everything?'

Uncle Wizard and Bob stood on The Witch's doorstep and checked their baggage. They had maps, spells, powders and potions, and quite the most delicious selection of pies.

'We're all set,' said Uncle Wizard. 'Are you sure you wont come with us?'

For a moment The Witch looked towards the dark rumbling clouds above the Hollow-Mountains, and then took a deep breath.

'I'm afraid I have something rather urgent to attend to, but I'm sure you'll be fine. And remember, only a wizard can defeat Grim Wizard. Good luck Uncle Wizard, I'll be thinking of you. Good luck too, Mr Bob.'

Uncle Wizard and Bob waved goodbye to The Witch. They walked down the garden path and then set off into the afternoon sunshine in search of the Thunder Troll.

It was getting late. Uncle Wizard and Bob had journeyed throughout the day and had now stopped for tea. Up ahead the path forked off in three different directions.

'So,' said Bob munching on a pie, 'which way is it to this Thunder Troll?'

Uncle Wizard unfolded the map.

'Well, we've got three choices. The shortest way is the first path...'

'Let's go that way,' said Bob eagerly.

'Right you are, the first path it is then,' said Uncle Wizard cheerily. 'Lets just hope the Fang-Beast isn't hungry when we cross the Swamp of Horror...'

Bob gulped nervously.

'On second thoughts, we'll take the second path.'

'Good choice,' said Uncle Wizard, 'the second path has the best scenery; the Starlight-Hills, Sparkle-River, Bliss Valley, the Jungle of Really Scary Things...'

'The Jungle of what?' gasped Bob.

'Oh yes, the Jungle of Really Scary Things has

some wonderful scenery…well apart from the five-headed spider-cows.'

Bob groaned.

'And the third path?'

Uncle Wizard studied the map.

'Yes, that way seems fine, no horror-swamps, no five-headed spider-cows.  There is a small hill we have to cross, but that shouldn't be too much trouble.'

Bob looked at Uncle Wizard dubiously.

'Are you sure you're telling me everything?'

'Oh yes,' said Uncle Wizard, 'its just a small hill.  Shouldn't be a problem…funny name, though. I wonder why its called *Haunted Hill*?'

'*Haunted Hill…*'

'Oh, I'm sure it will be fine.  Come on, lets go…'

Bob trudged despondently behind Uncle Wizard.  He scuffed his feet and muttered under his breath.  How had he got himself into this?  He should be at home eating pies, not heading down a path towards Haunted Hill.  He was sure something was going to eat him.

'Evening sirs…'

By a meadow, where mega-ducks slept in the swaying grass, an old farmer leant against a fence. He sucked on a length of straw and gazed up at the slowly darkening sky.

'And good evening to you, sir,' said Uncle Wizard.

The farmer shook his head knowledgably.

'Nay, it'll not be a good evening, sir.  Not with

that sky.'

Bob looked up at the sky.

'Why, what's wrong with it?'

The farmer did not answer.  He just shook his head sadly and mumbled something about turnips.

'Well, we wont keep you,' said Uncle Wizard. 'We're just off to Haunted Hill.'

The farmer's eyes shot wide open.

'Haunted Hill!  Haunted Hill!  You'll not be wanting to go to Haunted Hill.'

'Why ever not?' asked Uncle Wizard.

'Because it's haunted…by ghosts!'

Uncle Wizard laughed.

'That's all right,' he said, 'I don't believe in ghosts.'

'You will do,' said the farmer with a chuckle. 'Aye, you will do.'

Uncle Wizard and Bob left the farmer sucking on his straw and headed off towards Haunted Hill. On either side of the path a tall, shadowy forest rose up.  From out of the darkness came the cries and shrieks of beady-eyed creatures.  Guzzle-bats hung from the branches of blood-trees and skitter-lizards sniffed out grub-ants.

Up ahead the path turned left.  The trees thinned out and the ground began to rise. Hammered into the ground was a crooked sign that creaked in the wind.

It read 'Haunted Hill'.

Uncle Wizard and Bob gazed upwards.

'Aah,' said Uncle Wizard.

'Oh dear,' said Bob.

There it stood. Haunted Hill. A ghastly mound; wretched and miserable. On its summit stood a forest of fear-trees. Tangled branches swayed like clawing arms. Ghastly cries echoed on the wind.

'Still don't believe in ghosts?' asked Bob.

For a moment Uncle Wizard stared at the forest of fear-trees. Swirling mist filled the air. The moon slipped behind a cloud.

'Absolutely not. Come on, nothing to worry about. This way…'

Reluctantly Bob followed Uncle Wizard up the path that led to the top of Haunted Hill. No grass grew on the slopes. The soil was cracked and as black as night.

'Aaaaaaaaarrghhh,' cried Bob suddenly.

'What?' said Uncle Wizard.

'A ghost. I saw a ghost!'

'Where?'

'Up there, up there!' said Bob pointing at the trees.

Uncle Wizard stopped and peered into the darkness of the forest. There was nothing to see but a tangled mass of knotted branches.

'Its only shadows, Bob. Nothing to worry about.'

Soon they had climbed the hill and stood on the edge of the forest. A foul smell of decay filled the air.

'Now,' said Uncle Wizard looking at the map, 'we just walk through the forest and…'

'Aaaaaarrrgghh!' cried Bob. 'Another one!'

'Another what?'

'Another ghost!  All white and glowing it was.'

Uncle Wizard shook his head and peered into the gloom, but there was nothing to see except trees and swirling mist.

'Bob, there's no such things as ghosts.  Now come on, we're going in.'

Uncle Wizard brushed aside a curtain of creepers and led them into the forest of fear-trees. It was hopelessly dark.  The trees seemed to close in around them.  The undergrowth tugged at their feet.  As the path took them deeper into the forest strange cries echoed on the wind.

Bob was utterly terrified.

'We're going to get eaten!'

'Nonsense,' replied Uncle Wizard turning around to face Bob.  'How many times do I have to say it, there's no such things as ghosts.  They simply don't exist.'

Suddenly Bob's eyes bulged out of their sockets.  He stared straight ahead with a look of complete terror on his face.

'If ghosts don't exist,' he said with a whimper, 'then what's that?'

Uncle Wizard turned around.  There, stood in the middle of the path, was a ghost.  It was white and glowing and quite clearly a ghost.  The ghost screamed.  It was a horrifying sound.

For a moment Uncle Wizard stood rigidly still. He stared at the ghost, and slowly a look of utter astonishment appeared on his face.

'Now,' he said calmly, 'there's an entirely

rational explanation for this.'

'And what's that then?' asked Bob.

'Erm, I've been completely wrong. Quite clearly ghosts do exist. Look, they have giant fangs too.'

The ghost screamed and stumbled towards them. It's outstretched hands groped the air. Suddenly another ghost appeared, and then another. More stumbled out of the trees, hundreds of them. They blocked the path, and with their fangs glistening in the eerie light, grasped and wailed their way towards Uncle Wizard and Bob.

'Err, what's the plan?' asked Bob nervously.

Uncle Wizard backed away slowly. His head flitted from side to side. They were surrounded. The forest was alive with an army of ghosts.

'We've only one chance, we're going to run for it.'

'Good plan,' said Bob.

Uncle Wizard smiled.

'Yes, straight at the ghosts.'

'What?'

'Charge!'

Uncle Wizard let out a deafening cry and then charged at the ghosts, shouting and waving his arms like a madman.

For a second the ghosts were utterly startled. A crazy wailing wizard was hurtling towards them like an express train. Pandemonium erupted. First one ghost turned and fled and then another. Hundreds of terrified ghosts suddenly ran for it. They pushed and shoved. They elbowed and bumped, anything to get away from the crazy screaming wizard.

Bob was aghast.

'What are you doing?' he cried.

'I'm saving the world,' said Uncle Wizard.

'Not you're not, you're going mad.'

The ghosts fled along the path like a river of glowing white rushing towards a waterfall. Some ghosts dived into bushes and some hid behind trees. Some even burst into tears. Uncle Wizard tore after them, wailing and hooting, yelping and screaming.

Bob was distraught.

'We're going to get eaten!'

'Nonsense,' cried Uncle Wizard.

More and more ghosts dived into the darkest depths of the forest. They clambered over each other desperate to escape. Very soon there was not a single ghost to be seen.

'Look!' cried Uncle Wizard, 'the exit.'

Up ahead a ray of moonlight broke through the darkness. There was a gap in the trees where the path lead safely out of the forest.

'See,' said Uncle Wizard, slowing down, 'nothing to worry about. I had everything under control.'

'Stop right there!'

The most hideous voice imaginable echoed out of the darkness. Uncle Wizard and Bob froze on the spot. They watched in horror as a monstrous thing stepped out of the shadows and stood in the middle of the path. It was a Ghost-Giant, the ghastliest of all the ghosts. Worms wriggled through its nose and slime oozed from its scabby skin. It lifted a huge leg and took a pace towards them. As it touched a flower the petals turned to ash. With a sickening thud the Ghost-Giant stood before them.

'Erm, err,' spluttered Uncle Wizard with a gasp.

The Ghost-Giant's mouth squelched open. Three snake-tongues slithered in its mouth. The air froze.

'You will never leave Haunted Hill...'

Bob almost fainted. Uncle Wizard's knees turned to jelly. The Ghost-Giant fixed them with a stare from its blood-red eyes. Suddenly a huge beaming smile burst onto its face.

'…You will never leave Haunted Hill without a big thank you from me! All that chasing and screaming, what jolly good fun! It's really made our day! Normally people just run away from us ghosts. Let me shake you by the hand. Can we do it all again?'

Uncle Wizard breathed a huge sigh of relief.

'Would love to…' he said. 'Unfortunately I'm off to save the world. Perhaps another time?'

'Oh yes, yes, that would be super!' said the Ghost-Giant. 'Well, goodbye then.'

Uncle Wizard said goodbye to the Ghost-Giant and then he and Bob walked casually out of the forest of fear-trees, and safely down the other side of Haunted Hill.

# 8

Uncle Wizard and Bob sat on a rock at the bottom of Haunted Hill and took a well earned rest. The moon shone brightly and the stars twinkled like glistening crystals.

Uncle Wizard scratched his chin.

'It's getting late, we'll need to find somewhere to stay for the night...'

Suddenly Bob noticed something rather peculiar.

'Erm, we appear to be moving.'

Uncle Wizard could scarcely believe his eyes. They were waddling along the path on a giant rock.

'Oh, don't mind me,' said the waddling rock, 'I'm just on my way home to the Boom Mountains. Would you like a lift somewhere?'

Uncle Wizard bent over the front of the rock and came face to face with two lazy, timeless eyes. Beneath them a kindly mouth smiled in the moonlight.

'Well, that's very kind indeed. We're off to find the Thunder Troll, are you going anywhere near there?'

The rock pondered thoughtfully for a moment.

'Hmm, I can take you halfway there, but I do need to get back home. I have a wife and three pebbles to look after, you see.'

'That would be splendid!' said Uncle Wizard.

The waddling rock shuffled along the path. It was not a very talkative rock so Uncle Wizard and Bob sat back and admired the scenery. They saw a shooting-starfish go skidding across the sky, and caught a glimpse of an undercover-gnu lurking in the shadows of a spy-tree.

'What's that over there?' asked Bob suddenly.

The waddling rock raised its stony eyebrows. Over in a field a herd of camels were eagerly digging holes in the ground. They would peer excitingly into the freshly dug holes as if searching for something, but then mutter disappointedly to one another.

'They're moon-camels,' said the rock slowly.

'What are they looking for?' asked Bob.

'The moon.'

'The moon? Don't they know it's in the sky?'

The waddling rock sighed.

'We have tried telling them but they wont listen.'

Eventually they came to a fork in the path. With a judder the waddling rock came to a halt and Uncle Wizard and Bob climbed off.

'Sorry I can't take you all the way,' said the rock, 'but I do need to get back. My dinner will be waiting, it's fissures 'n bricks tonight...'

The waddling rock said goodbye and then trundled off home to the Boom Mountains.

Uncle Wizard and Bob waved goodbye and then walked along the path until they came to a leafy glade by a burbling river. They made a bed of moss under a lullaby-tree and then snuggled down for the night.

'Quite a day,' said Uncle Wizard.

'Quite a day,' agreed Bob with a giant yawn and then promptly fell asleep.

For a while Uncle Wizard stared up at the stars. He was enjoying saving the world. He knew there would be danger, he knew Grim Wizard was after him, but as the lullaby-tree sung him gently to sleep he smiled at all the excitement of his wonderful adventure.

# 9

The Land of Forever sparkled in the morning sunshine. Mega-toads croaked, natter-cats chatted and out in the fields danger-chickens scavenged for their morning feed.

Bob woke with a yawn and a stretch.

'Another day, another pie…'

'No time for breakfast,' said Uncle Wizard who was busy studying the map, 'we need to get moving.'

Bob was aghast.

'No breakfast! I need my morning pie. Doctor's orders.'

Uncle Wizard looked dubious.

'Are you sure a doctor ordered you to eat pies?'

Bob tugged at his bobble hat uneasily.

'Well, I think he was a doctor…although, now you come to mention it he did look uncannily like Mr Wobble of *Wobble's Pie Shop*…'

Uncle Wizard shook his head in dismay.

'Come on, this way…'

They packed up their things and followed the path through the leafy glade and down to the river. It was a crisp morning. The air was fresh and the grass sparkled with dew. High up in the Boom Mountains melting snow trickled into streams and fed the gushing river which flowed powerfully past the leafy glade.

Uncle Wizard tapped the map and sighed.

'We've got a good few hours walk ahead of us today. We follow the river down to Draggle Canyon. Hmm…if only we had a boat…'

Suddenly his eyes lit up. A huge beaming smile burst out across his face and he threw up his arms in delight.

'I have it! A spell. I can make a boat with a spell…!'

Bob groaned.

'Do you have to? Something's bound to explode.'

Uncle Wizard shook his head.

'What could possibly explode?'

Bob looked at the gushing river and sighed.

'Probably everything…'

Uncle Wizard tutted and waved Bob away. He

took a deep breath and concentrated hard. How difficult could a boat spell be? From the pockets of his magic cloak he pulled out his powders and potions. There was slurp-weed and grumble-rain, zoink-powder and flabble-juice. He poured the whole lot into his magic hat and then pulled out a giant bottle of whiz-bang powder.

'One boat coming up…'

The spell began to gargle and fizz. With a steady hand Uncle Wizard measured out a spoonful of whiz-bang powder and held it over his magic hat.

'It's going to explode,' said Bob, who hid behind a rock with his wings over his eyes.

'Nothing's going to explode, trust me.'

'Trust you!' exclaimed Bob, 'the last time you said that you turned me into a giant turnip.'

The spell was a swirling tornado of spitting, sparkling colours. Flashes of light leapt out of the magic-hat and made the air sizzle with electric-rainbows. Uncle Wizard steadied himself and poured in the whiz-bang powder.

And nothing happened…

There was no bang, no explosion and certainly no boat. The spell gurgled for a second and then went *plop!*

Uncle Wizard was aghast.

'*Plop!* It shouldn't have just gone *plop*.'

Bob breathed a sigh of relief.

'Don't underestimate a *plop*. I'm quite happy with a *plop*. Nothing exploded and no one's been turned into a turnip. This could be your most successful spell ever!'

Uncle Wizard shrugged his shoulders.

'Oh well, looks like we're walking, come on, this way...'

'Erm, what's that noise?' said Bob with a nervous look on his face.

They both stood perfectly still and listened. Below the sound of the rushing water came a faint cracking sound. Ominously it grew louder and louder. Suddenly the ground shuddered like an earthquake. Uncle Wizard and Bob desperately clung to one another whilst all around them trees and bushes shook violently.

'You've really done it this time!' cried Bob.

From below the rushing waters of the river came a hideous grating sound. It scraped and jarred, clunked and jolted. It was as if the Land of Forever was tearing itself apart.

'All it did was go *plop!"* protested Uncle Wizard.

Bob gasped.

'I can't believe it! You're *plops* are worse than your explosions.'

The ground bounced like a hyper-trampoline. Snooze-monkeys were hurled out of lullaby-trees and all the fruit from the blubber-bush landed on the floor with a splat. Uncle Wizard and Bob were thrown this way and that. They bounced and lurched until finally the ground stopped shaking and they came to a rest at the edge of the river.

'Aah,' said Uncle Wizard.

'Oh dear,' said Bob.

There was something terribly wrong with the

river. It had stopped dead. Its gushing, winding waters had frozen solid. From the top of the Boom Mountains to the giant waterfall of Draggle Canyon, the river had turned to ice. Not a single drop of water moved, not a single twig drifted by.

Uncle Wizard buried his head in his hands.

'That really wasn't meant to happen.'

In frustration he kicked a pebble. The pebble landed on the river and slipped and skidded on the glistening ice until it disappeared from view.

Uncle Wizard raised his eyebrows.

'Hmm, I wonder…'

Gingerly he tapped the river with his toe. The ice was thick and slippery. He tried his other foot. The river easily held his weight.

'I have it! We can slide to Draggle Canyon,' he exclaimed. 'We'll be there in no time!'

Bob stared at Uncle Wizard in disbelief.

'Of all your crazy ideas, this is…'

But Bob never finished his words. Uncle Wizard scooped him up, sprinted as fast as he could and leapt onto the river of ice.

'Wooooooooooooh!' cried Uncle Wizard.

'Aaaaaaarrrghhhhh!' screamed Bob.

Uncle Wizard's feet landed on the ice. He flapped and flailed and just managed to keep his balance. Quickly they picked up speed. Uncle Wizard's boots skated over the ice like a racing toboggan. Trees whizzed past and bushes became a blur. They rocketed along on a river of ice, headed straight for Draggle Canyon.

'I'm not going to forgive you for this,' said Bob.

The river weaved this way and that. Uncle Wizard leant his body to steer round the bends and at one point even hurdled a frozen log. Suddenly the river cascaded down a hill and became a thundering ice-slide. Uncle Wizard and Bob were zooming along so fast their cheeks wobbled.

'How much further?' screamed Bob.

The rush of the wind was deafening.

'There's a tunnel in Draggle Canyon,' shouted Uncle Wizard. 'That's where we're heading. We need to get off this river just before it plunges off the waterfall.'

Bob nodded, then suddenly began to panic.

'Erm, how exactly are we going to stop?'

Uncle Wizard scratched his head.

'Aah, I hadn't thought of that.'

Faster and faster they went. The river began to widen and looming larger and larger was the mighty waterfall of Draggle Canyon. It was incredible. A mammoth, colossal waterfall. The frozen river tumbled over the edge and disappeared into the darkness of a bottomless pit.

Bob tugged Uncle Wizard's sleeve.

'Stop! Stop! You've got to make us stop!'

Uncle Wizard dug his boots deep into the ice but it did nothing to slow them down. They hurtled towards the edge of the waterfall without a chance of stopping.

'We're going to fall!' cried Bob.

Once more Uncle Wizard tried to stop. He jammed his boots into the ice and flapped his arms like a windmill.

'It's not working,' screamed Bob. 'We're doomed!'

The waterfall was upon them. The deep, dark abyss of the bottomless pit seemed to be sucking them in.

'Do something,' pleaded Bob, 'anything. There must be something in your cloak.'

Uncle Wizard looked all around. There was nothing to save them. No trees to grab hold of, no bushes to stop them. Suddenly he had an idea.

'I've got it!'

Bob's eyes lit up with hope.

'What's the plan?' he cried eagerly.

Uncle Wizard took a deep breath and turned to face Bob.

'I'm going to take off my clothes...'

'What!' screamed Bob incredulously, 'we're about to fall off the edge of a waterfall into a bottomless pit and your plan is to take off your clothes?'

'Exactly,' said Uncle Wizard calmly.

Bob's eyes popped out of his head.

'You've gone mad! You're utterly insane.'

'Maybe...but maybe it might just work.'

'And what if it doesn't?' cried Bob.

Uncle Wizard looked at the waterfall, it was just seconds away. He then wriggled out of his magic cloak and smiled.

'Then we're doomed…'

Bob opened his mouth to scream, but it was too late. The river of ice ended and Uncle Wizard and Bob plunged over the edge of the giant waterfall.

# 10

'Aaaarrrrgggghh!'

Bob screamed at the top of his voice as they plunged over the edge of the waterfall. 'We're doomed…'

The waterfall dropped away into the deepest darkest depths. Desperately Bob groped for the edge, anything to cling onto, but there was nothing to save them. The only way was down.

'Aaaarrrrgggghh,' he screamed again.

Uncle Wizard waited for a moment then coughed politely.

'Bob, I don't mean to interrupt, but…'

'Not now,' cried Bob, 'can't you see I'm busy falling to my doom…hang on a minute, something's not right…'

Bob looked around in utter amazement. Nothing had happened. They were suspended in mid-air above the waterfall. They should have plummeted like a stone, but if anything they were going up. They were flying!

Uncle Wizard smiled.

'Welcome to Wizard Air. Please fasten your seat-belts. We hope you enjoy the flight.'

Bob looked up. Above them, fluttering in the wind was Uncle Wizard's magic cloak. It had grown to the size of a giant hand-glider, and was lifting them away from the plunging waterfall. With a gentle tug on the cloak's sleeves Uncle Wizard turned them around, and catching a hearty gust of wind they glided through Draggle Canyon.

'See,' said Uncle Wizard, 'never in any danger.'

Far below were boulders and trees and the occasional sun-lizard scrabbling over the craggy rocks. A troupe of bumble-monkeys waved to them from the shade of a giant fern.

'Well, this is pleasant,' said Uncle Wizard cheerily.

Bob shook his head in disbelief.

'Pleasant? I'm flying through a canyon with a crazy wizard wearing just his underpants! Nothing about this is pleasant!'

'Now, now Bob, calm down. The tunnel we're heading for is just along here. We'll be there in no time.'

Uncle Wizard pulled left and they swooped closer to the towering cliff face, which rose up from the canyon floor. In a crevice they saw a wind-worm nesting on eggs and a hover-dog nibbling a bone. They even caught sight of a bungee-bug leaping off the cliff face, only to spring back up on its elastic legs.

Suddenly Uncle Wizard's eyes lit up.

'Look, there it is, down there. The tunnel...!'

Down below, carved into the rock face was the entrance to the tunnel. Uncle Wizard tugged on the sleeves of his magic cloak and slowly they began to descend.

'I had a look at the map this morning,' said Uncle Wizard excitedly. 'The Lair of the Thunder Troll is at the end of this tunnel. It wont be long before we have the first part of the spell!'

With a gentle bump they came to rest safely on the canyon floor.

'Now, that wasn't so bad, was it?' said Uncle Wizard as he put his magic cloak back on.

Bob stared at him in disbelief.

'Not so bad!' he exclaimed, 'I've been hurled along a river of ice and I've plunged over an enormous waterfall. I tell you, I'll be glad when we get inside this tunnel.'

Uncle Wizard nodded.

'Yes, perhaps you're right.  I'm sure we'll be much safer then.  I mean, what could possibly happen to us inside the Tunnel of Terror?'

Bob gasped.

'The Tunnel of what!' he exclaimed.

'Oh don't worry, I'm sure it'll be fine.'

# 11

The Tunnel of Terror was cold and damp. Uncle Wizard lit a candle and they set off into the flickering darkness.

It was slow going. Giant spider-webs stretched across the tunnel, and flocks of flapping bats burst out of the darkness. The deeper they went, the more treacherous it became. Water dripped from the ceiling and the floor was covered in foul-smelling sludge.

'I'm not enjoying this,' said Bob.

Uncle Wizard raised his eyebrows.

'Why ever not?'

Bob looked fearfully around the Tunnel of Terror. From every crag of rock ominous eyes blinked back at him.

'Well, it's dark, we don't know where we're going, and there's probably a hundred things down here that want to eat us.'

'Nonsense Bob, who would want to eat us?'

Suddenly a terrible moan echoed through the tunnel.

'Well, there's something for a start,' said Bob.

'Now Bob, let's not be hasty. Just because we're in a dark sinister tunnel with some sort of groaning monster, doesn't necessarily mean we're in danger...'

Just then the light from Uncle Wizard's candle lit up a sign on the wall. The sign read:

*'You Are Doomed!'*

'On the other hand we could be in a whole heap of trouble…'

They struggled deeper into the darkness. Suddenly the moan sounded again, much nearer this time. It was a desperate, harrowing sound. Uncle Wizard and Bob edged cautiously round a bend in the tunnel when suddenly they came across a sight that took their breath away. Before them, enormous beyond belief, was a vast underground cavern. The whole of Wizard HQ could have fitted inside. Flickering torches lit up the cavern, and from one side to the other stretched a deep, dark lake.

'What is this place?' asked Bob nervously.

Uncle Wizard looked at the map.

'I think this is the Cavern of Peril…'

Suddenly a terrible moan echoed through the cavern. On the far side of the lake sat a blob. It was the most miserable looking blob imaginable. It had two sad eyes and a sagging face.

'Oh, woe and doom!' the blob cried sorrowfully, 'there's people in my cavern! You've come to make Gloom the Blob happy, haven't you? I can't stand being happy. I'd rather hit myself over the head with a wooden spoon than be happy…would you like me to hit myself over the head with a wooden spoon?'

Uncle Wizard looked rather puzzled.

'Erm, I don't think we need you to do that…'

'Really, its no bother.'

Gloom let out a terrible sigh, then picked up a wooden spoon and began to hit himself over the head.

Uncle Wizard and Bob looked at one another.

'There's a possibility,' said Uncle Wizard in a confidential whisper, 'that Gloom is quite, quite mad.'

Bob nodded.

'That is one odd blob.'

As Gloom carried on hitting himself over the head, Uncle Wizard stared at the lake. The water was calm, but now and then it would ripple as if deep below the surface strange creatures prowled the depths. He scratched his head thoughtfully. They needed to cross the lake. It was the only way to reach the Lair of the Thunder Troll.

'If only there was a bridge,' he said with a sigh, 'we'd be across in seconds…that's it, a bridge! A bridge to cross the lake!'

Bob looked anxious.

'And where are we going to get a bridge from?'

Uncle Wizard beamed.

'I know just the spell!'

'Not another one?' groaned Bob. 'Haven't you done enough damage for one day?'

But Uncle Wizard was already flicking through the pages of his spell book.

'Aah yes, page 42, gigantic-bridge spell. Now, what do I need?'

He unscrewed bottles and opened leather pouches. Into his magic hat went a dab of bubble-jinx, three ping-pong puddles and a sprinkle of zoom-dust. He gave the spell a shake. It coughed and spluttered and then gave off a great flash of light. Suddenly the ground began to shake.

'And now,' he said eagerly, 'how much whiz-bang powder do I need?'

He read the spell, paused, then read it again.

'That can't be right, no whiz-bang powder! Oh well, I'm sure a drop or two wont hurt...'

Then came the explosion.

The Cavern of Peril leapt ten feet off the ground then crashed back down with a bone-shattering thud. There were flames and smoke everywhere. Uncle Wizard looked on expectantly as the air cleared, but the spell had been a disaster. Instead of a gigantic-bridge stretching across the lake, there was, sat at the water's edge, simply a plain old fridge.

'Well,' said Bob with a sigh, 'even by your standards that was really terrible.'

Uncle Wizard shook his head disappointedly.

'I can't have used enough whiz-bang

powder...'

Over on the other side of the lake Gloom the Blob had stopped hitting himself over the head with the wooden spoon. As the smoke cleared from Uncle Wizard's spell, a mischievous glint appeared in his eye.

'Oh, woe and doom!' he cried dismally, 'I suppose you'll be wanting to use my boat now...'

Uncle Wizard looked up hopefully.

'There's a boat?'

Something approaching a smile appeared on Gloom's face. It was crafty and cunning. He pointed across the lake.

'Behind that rock. You can use it to cross the lake. Only don't try to make me happy when you get here. I couldn't stand being happy...'

Uncle Wizard and Bob rushed over to the rock. Behind it, tethered to a stake, a rowing boat bobbed gently in the water. Two oars sat ready and waiting.

'Well, this is perfect,' said Uncle Wizard.

Quickly Uncle Wizard untied the boat and then he and Bob jumped in. With a hearty push on the rock they sent themselves bobbing across the lake.

'Well, this is the life,' said Uncle Wizard as he took up the oars and began rowing.

On the other side of the lake Gloom the Blob had shuffled towards the water's edge. As he watched the ripples and splashes on the surface of the lake, the something on his face which looked like a smile got wider and wider. Bob stared at him suspiciously.

'Something's bothering me,' he said.

The lake had began to froth and bubble. Gloom the Blob was slapping his sides with eager excitement.

'What's that?' asked Uncle Wizard.

Bob tugged at his bobble hat thoughtfully.

'Well, why is this place called the Cavern of Peril? It's not exactly terrifying, is it?'

'Hmm,' said Uncle Wizard, 'good point. I'll have a look at the map…'

He reached inside his magic cloak and pulled out the map. He studied it carefully, and then nodded knowledgeably.

'Simple really,' he said casually. 'It's called the Cavern of Peril because it's the home of the…oh my, oh no, were doomed!...Abandon Ship!!!'

Without a second thought Uncle Wizard grabbed Bob and leapt into the water. With desperate strokes he swam for the shore. Behind them the water churned and frothed as if an earthquake was erupting below the surface. On the other side of the lake Gloom bounced up and down in a frenzy.

'Eat them! Eat them!' he cried.

Suddenly a great hole appeared in the water. It was as if the lake was collapsing in on itself. The water churned and bubbled, and then, with a hideous, deafening roar, a grotesque head burst out of the water.

'What…what's that?' gasped Bob.

Uncle Wizard did not dare to turn round. He desperately swam for the water's edge.

'That's a Water Dragon!'

The Water Dragon roared. It's mouth snapped open. Lines of razor sharp teeth glinted in the cavern light. In a flash it had bitten the boat in half.

Gloom the Blob howled with laughter.

'Eat them! Eat them!' he cried.

The Water Dragon's blazing red eyes settled on the frantically splashing figures. It bellowed with all its fury, bared its teeth, and then dived through the water towards them. And as Uncle Wizard groped despairingly for the water's edge, all Bob could do was scream…

# 12

Gloom the Blob wailed with manic laughter. It's blubbery body bounced up and down as the Water Dragon streaked through the water.

'Oh woe and doom!' he cried, 'they're going to get eaten, and that will make me happy…oh well, I'll just have to be happy.'

Uncle Wizard struggled through the water. His feet splashed desperately and his hands grasped for the shore. Bob clung to his back as behind them the Water Dragon roared mercilessly.

'Faster!' he cried despairingly.

'Eat them! Eat them! ' cried Gloom.

The Water Dragon opened its mouth. Steam poured out of its nostrils. Its giant claws crashed through the water and its eyes boiled a furious red.

'Almost there!' screamed Bob.

Uncle Wizard kicked his legs and desperately ploughed through the water. Suddenly his feet touched the bottom. With his final ounce of strength he stood up, waded through the water and then collapsed in a heap as he reached dry land.

'Erm,' said Bob nervously, 'do you want the bad news, or the very bad news…'

Uncle Wizard groaned and lifted his head. The Water Dragon was still after them. It powered through the water like a rocket fish. Suddenly two flaming balls of fire blasted out of its nostrils. Uncle Wizard and Bob just managed to duck as they slammed into the cavern wall.

With aching muscles Uncle Wizard hauled himself to his feet. He stood with his hands on his hips and tried to catch his breath. As he did so the Water Dragon burst out of the lake. Its razor claws dug into the shore and its huge scaly body pulled itself out of the water.

'Erm,' said Bob nervously, 'are you any good at Water Dragon taming?'

Uncle Wizard shook his head.

'Well, I'm not exactly a professional...run!'

They turned to run, but as they did so they clattered straight into the plain old fridge and collapsed in a heap. The fridge rocked back and forth. As it settled it began to make a bizarre humming sound. Without warning the fridge then leapt into the air as if it were a pogo-stick.

'How odd,' said Uncle Wizard.

The fridge shot off towards the cavern roof, hung in mid-air for a second, and then landed back on the ground with a thud. Uncle Wizard's eyes began to twinkle. Perhaps his spell had not been a complete disaster.

'It's not a gigantic bridge,' he cried in delight, 'it's a bionic fridge! Bob, I have an idea. Quick, after that fridge!'

The fridge bounced about the cavern like a jack-in-the-box whilst Uncle Wizard scrambled after it. He leapt and dived and landed flat on his face until finally he grabbed hold of it with his fingernails. Bob was dumbfounded.

'What are you doing?'

'Come on,' said Uncle Wizard, 'climb onboard.'

'I'm not climbing on that...'

But as he spoke the cavern echoed to the sound of the Water Dragon's roar. Without another thought Bob clambered aboard the fridge.

'What's the plan?'

'Erm...duck!'

But it was too late. The Water Dragon blasted two fire-balls straight at them. They were certain to be burnt to a crisp when suddenly the fridge leapt high into the air and the bolts of fire sizzled by harmlessly beneath them.

'Wooooooooooh!' cried Uncle Wizard.

'Aaaaaarrrgghh!' screamed Bob.

The fridge landed at the back of the cavern.

'I wonder,' said Uncle Wizard scratching his chin, 'with enough of a run up, can a bionic-fridge jump over a lake?'

'You're not serious are you?' said Bob quivering.

'Oh yes,' said Uncle Wizard with a huge beaming smile, 'absolutely serious…'

The Water Dragon hauled itself completely out of the water. It stood on the shore, directly in front of the fridge. Over on the other side of the lake Gloom the Blob waved his wooden spoon excitedly.

'Oh woe and doom!' he wailed, 'I'm about to be very happy. Who will get eaten first?'

Uncle Wizard took a deep breath.

'All set?'

Bob shook his head.

'No. This is utter madness!'

'Or maybe its genius?' said Uncle Wizard smiling.

'No, no,' said Bob, 'trying to jump over a lake on a bionic-fridge with a Water Dragon waiting to eat you is definitely madness. Now, a never-ending pie, that would be genius…'

'We'll see. Yee-hah!'

As if he were riding a horse Uncle Wizard gave the fridge a good hard kick. The fridge jolted, juddered, and then bounded towards the lake. Faster and faster it went. The Water Dragon stood before them. Its nostrils flickered with flame. It threw back its head, and then blasted a stream of raging fire at the bounding fridge.

'Aargh!' screamed Uncle Wizard.

'Aaaaaarrrgghh!' screamed Bob.

Just at the last second, the fridge leapt into the air. It leapt high over the fire, high over the Water Dragon and high over the lake.

'Wooooooooooh!' cried Uncle Wizard.

'Aaaaaarrrgghh!' screamed Bob.

The wind rushed past as they flew through the air. Down below the Water Dragon roared.

'This is splendid!' exclaimed Uncle Wizard.

'This is madness!' cried Bob.

The fridge soared to the top of the cavern. It was halfway across the lake. Down below the Water Dragon twisted its neck and reared up on its hind legs. Volley after volley of flaming fire-balls shot towards the fridge. The air was alive with fire. The fridge swerved and dipped, it swayed and veered, desperately avoiding the fire-balls. Some sizzled past their heads. Some crashed into the cavern wall.

'We're doomed!' cried Bob.

The fridge arced through the air. It began to descend to the other side of the lake. With a final, terrifying cry of rage the Water Dragon ripped two chunks of rock out of the floor. It hurled them at the fridge.

'Look out!' cried Uncle Wizard.

But it was too late. With a terrible crash the fridge was hit. It buckled, jerked, and went into a dizzying spin. Uncle Wizard and Bob were thrown clear. With flailing arms and desperate cries they plunged towards the cavern floor.

'Woe and tragedy!' cried Gloom, 'nothing can save you now…'

The fridge crashed to the ground. It fell onto jagged rocks and was smashed to pieces. Uncle Wizard and Bob tumbled like rag-dolls. The cavern floor rushed towards them. Gloom shrieked in delight.

'You've had it, you're doomed, you're…oh no!'

Gloom let out a gasp as he realised what was about to happen. He tried to wriggle away, but was too slow. Uncle Wizard and Bob fell out of the air and with a hearty squelch landed on Gloom's blubbery body. They bounced off the blob and found themselves standing safely on the cavern floor.

Gloom groaned. He stared at them with a look of utter despair on his face. He was about to speak, then just shrugged and began to hit himself over the head with his wooden spoon.

'Well,' said Uncle Wizard with a big beaming smile, 'we can't hang around here all day. We've got a world to save.'

He tipped his hat to the Water Dragon, patted Gloom on the shoulder and then set off with Bob down the tunnel towards the Lair of the Thunder Troll.

# 13

Uncle Wizard and Bob set off towards the Lair of the Thunder Troll. A chill wind blew. Two-headed mud-snakes slithered through the sludge on the tunnel floor.

'Are you sure this is the right way?'

Bob clung nervously to Uncle Wizard. Every flicker of candle light on the jagged walls made him flinch. Uncle Wizard peered closely at the map.

'The Thunder Troll lives at the end of the tunnel. There's still a way to go yet.'

On and on they trudged. The Tunnel of Terror seemed endless. Bones crunched under their feet and the glowing eyes of flame-bats glinted in the darkness. Now and then distant cries echoed through the tunnel. There were howls and screams and then worst of all, a final, hopeless silence.

Abruptly Uncle Wizard came to a halt. He studied the map and took a deep breath.

'I think we're nearly there, look…'

Before them, sloping ominously downwards was a series of steps carved into the rock. They descended into a gloomy, swirling darkness.

Bob gulped.

'And I guess we have to go down there?'

Uncle Wizard was silent for a moment. He peered into the cold, swirling mists below and then turned to Bob.

'Well, as I see it we've got two options. Firstly we can set off down these steps and face the

Thunder Troll…'

Bob nodded anxiously.

'…or we can stand here and get eaten by the giant dagger-rat which seems to have crept up behind us.'

Bob turned around slowly. There, gnashing its teeth in the flickering shadows, was a giant dagger-rat. Its eyes were slime green, and its body was thick with bristly hair. It flicked out its tongue and almost slurped Bob into its huge slavering mouth.

'Hmm,' said Bob, edging nervously away, 'I think now would be a good time to run away, excuse me…'

Bob took a deep breath, let out a terrified scream and then hurtled down the steps as fast as he could run. Uncle Wizard eventually caught up with him halfway down the steps. He was huddled in a shadow and wheezing for breath.

'Did it, follow us?' asked Bob fearfully.

Uncle Wizard smiled and shook his head.

'Of course not. Dagger-rats aren't stupid you know. There's a Thunder Troll down here, you'd have to be mad to come this way…'

Uncle Wizard patted Bob on the head and then set off down the craggy steps, into the cold grey mist below. The wind began to bite. A foul stench filled the air. It was the smell of rotten meat crawling with a million ugly maggots.

Bob had been thinking.

'Err, how exactly do you get a tooth from a Thunder Troll?'

Uncle Wizard smiled.

'I have a plan!'

'What sort of plan?' asked Bob anxiously.

Uncle Wizard stopped and took a deep breath. He turned to Bob.

'Honestly, it's probably the worst plan I've ever had. It's a terrible plan; awful, appalling, but…'

'But what?' exclaimed Bob.

'…but,' said Uncle Wizard with a wink, 'it might just work. Come on, I can smell the breath of a Thunder Troll.'

They descended the last few steps. The mist parted, and before them, as dark as the cruellest night, was the Lair of the Thunder Troll.

'Aah,' said Uncle Wizard.

'Oh dear,' said Bob.

Nothing could have prepared them for the sight before their eyes. There was no floor. A great chasm fell away beneath them. Across the chasm stretched a wooden bridge tethered at each end by thickly coiled rope. On the bridge stood a beast from the most hideous nightmare.

'Crikes!' exclaimed Uncle Wizard.

'Crumbs alive!' exclaimed Bob.

The Thunder Troll bellowed into the cold dark air and beat its fists against its chest. The sound was like thunder. Chunks of rock plummeted into the chasm below. The Thunder Troll took two paces forward. The bridge creaked under the weight of its clumping feet.

'So what's the plan?' asked Bob nervously. 'What spell is it this time?'

'No spell,' said Uncle Wizard calmly.

Bob looked anxious.

'No spell? Are you serious? That's a Thunder Troll standing there. Look at its claws! How are you going to get one of its teeth?'

Uncle Wizard cleared his throat.

'Simple...I'm going to ask it very nicely.'

Bob was stunned. He could not believe his ears.

'What?'

'I'm going to ask the Thunder Troll very nicely if I can have one of its teeth.'

Bob's mouth fell open.

'That's your plan? Have you been at the Wizard Juice again? This is madness. That Thunder Troll is ten-foot tall and invincible and you're just going to ask for one of its teeth?'

'Oh, I'm sure it wont mind. Its probably got plenty of teeth to spare.'

Just then the Thunder Troll opened its mouth.

'Aah,' said Uncle Wizard.

'Oh dear,' said Bob.

In the middle of the Thunder Troll's huge mouth there was a single tooth, no more, no less. It sat like a prized possession, razor-sharp and gleaming. Gently the Thunder Troll stroked the tooth and then stared at Uncle Wizard with menacing eyes. Bob gasped and dived underneath Uncle Wizard's cloak.

'I can't watch, we're done for!'

Uncle Wizard looked at the Thunder Troll for a moment and then shrugged.

'Oh well,' he said, 'I suppose you can only ask.'

He took a pace forward and smiled at the Thunder Troll.

'Good day, sir. My name is Uncle Wizard. Now, I know this may sound rather odd, and normally I wouldn't dream of asking a Thunder Troll this, but could I possibly have your tooth please?'

For a moment the Lair of the Thunder Troll fell silent. The bridge swayed silently above the dark, infinite chasm.

'How's it going?' asked Bob nervously from underneath the magic cloak.

Uncle Wizard stood on the bridge and scratched his chin thoughtfully.

'There are some positives,' he said slowly.

'Such as?'

'Well, it hasn't eaten me yet.'

Suddenly the Thunder Troll let out a terrifying bellow. It threw up its arms and then charged across the bridge, straight at Uncle Wizard.

'I'll take that as a no then...'

# 14

The Thunder Troll charged at Uncle Wizard. Its huge feet pounded across the bridge and its eyes blazed with raging-fire.

'Run!' cried Bob, 'run for your life.'

The Thunder Troll roared and the bridge shook.

'Run!' screamed Bob again. 'We'll be trampled to death!'

But something had caught Uncle Wizard's eye. He stood directly in the path of the Thunder Troll and held out his hand as if he were directing traffic.

'Stop,' he said simply.

The Thunder Troll snarled. Smoke and fire bellowed out of its nostrils. With every crashing step the bridge swayed more violently.

Still Uncle Wizard did not move.

'Stop,' he said again.

Bob was frantic. They would be squashed under the Thunder Troll's foot or thrown into the chasm below.

The Thunder Troll raised it arms. Huge pulsing muscles rippled under its ragged clothes. Razor sharp claws slashed the air. It was now halfway across the bridge!

'Run!' pleaded Bob desperately. 'Run, now!'

But still Uncle Wizard stood his ground. He faced the Thunder Troll with his hand held out.

'Stop,' he said, 'please, stop...'

He then pointed at the Thunder Troll's foot.

'Your shoe...'

Bob gasped. They were about to get trampled to death by a ten-foot Thunder Troll, but all Uncle Wizard cared about was its shoe.

'Have you gone completely mad?' he cried in despair. 'We're here to save the world...not give out fashion tips. We need its tooth!'

Uncle Wizard turned to Bob.

'But it's shoelace is undone...it might trip over and hurt itself.'

Uncle Wizard turned back to face the Thunder Troll and once more pleaded with it to stop. He pointed at its shoelace, but the Thunder Troll just beat its chest and roared with fury as it pounded across the bridge.

Bob was desperate. He yanked at Uncle Wizard's cloak. He kicked his leg, but nothing would make him move.

The Thunder Troll was only paces away. One mighty crash on the bridge followed another. It was so close they could hear its furious wheezing and smell its putrid breath. The Thunder Troll raised its slashing claws and opened its slavering mouth. Its single, deadly tooth glistened like a sparkling sun.

'We're done for,' screamed Bob.

But even as the shadow of the Thunder Troll fell over them, still Uncle Wizard did not move. He looked at the Thunder Troll with pleading eyes and pointed one last time at its flapping shoelace.

'Please, look out, you're going to…'

'Grrraaaaagghhh!'

The Thunder Troll stepped on its shoelace.

The floor disappeared from under its feet. It let out a despairing cry and then tumbled through the air in a jumble of arms and legs. Desperately it tried to break its fall, but all it could do was scream in vain.

It hit the ground with a crunch. Its big bulbous head slammed hard into the bridge. As it did so there was a tiny, clinking crack. The Thunder Troll's tooth snapped off. It shot out of its mouth, spiralled through the air and landed gently in the outstretched hands of Uncle Wizard.

Bob's mouth dropped open in astonishment. He was speechless. He stood on the bridge and shook his head in disbelief.

Uncle Wizard held the shiny tooth aloft.

'One tooth of a Thunder Troll,' he cried proudly. 'We really are going to save the world!'

He put the tooth safely in his pocket and stepped over the groaning heap of the Thunder Troll. At the far end of the bridge daylight burst into the darkness. With a skip in his stride and a smile on his face, Uncle Wizard led Bob across the bridge and out into the brilliant sunshine beyond.

# 15

Uncle Wizard and Bob stepped out of the Tunnel of Terror and stood blinking in the dazzling sunshine. The Land of Forever shone like a glitter-angel's eye. The sky was electric-blue and the grass shimmered emerald-green.

'My, haven't you done well.'

Uncle Wizard gasped. He could barely believe his eyes. Sat on a blanket surrounded by the most sumptuous looking picnic was The Witch.

'Well, let me see it then.'

For a moment Uncle Wizard was overwhelmed. The Witch looked absolutely beautiful. She wore a long flowing dress and had bright red ribbons tied in her golden hair. Uncle Wizard pinched himself and then proudly pulled the Thunder Troll's gleaming tooth out of his pocket.

'Well done,' said The Witch proudly, 'I knew you could do it.'

Bob only had eyes for the picnic. There were mega-pies, sticky-buns and gooey-cakes galore. The Witch smiled.

'Please, Mr Bob, tuck in.'

Bob dived into a chocolate cake as if it were a swimming pool. Uncle Wizard sat down next to The Witch. He was just about to tell her about their battle with the Water Dragon when suddenly The Witch sighed deeply.

'What's the matter?' asked Uncle Wizard.

For a moment The Witch was silent.

'After you left my cottage I went to speak to some of my oldest friends in the Land of Forever. They told me of strange goings-on. A great evil has entered our land. People have disappeared, and ghastly creatures prowl the skies.'

'Grim Wizard?' asked Uncle Wizard.

The Witch looked to the far horizon.

'He has not been seen yet, but it is only a matter of time. He knows you are here. He will do anything to stop you.'

Uncle Wizard fell silent. He had been so wrapped up in finding the tooth of the Thunder Troll he had barely thought about Grim Wizard.

'What should I do?' he asked.

'Grim Wizard must be stopped at all costs. His evil is spreading. I will come with you on your adventure, at least until you find the second part of the Spell of Forever.'

Uncle Wizard's eyes lit up.

'That would be splendid!'

Suddenly he remembered the scroll. He pulled it from his pocket and carefully unrolled it. There before his eyes was the second part of the spell, but as before it was utterly confusing.

## *Fa E Laan*

Suddenly the air began to glow with magical fizzing sparkles. They fluttered like glittering dust and swathed the scroll in crystal light. Slowly the letters of the spell began to rearrange themselves.

Uncle Wizard looked on expectantly, eager to

learn what the second part of the spell would be. Finally the letters came to a rest.

Uncle Wizard read the spell.

'I don't understand,' he said with a confused look on his face.

Bob looked up from the pie he was devouring.

'What is it?' he asked.

Uncle Wizard shrugged.

'The next part of the spell, all we need is a leaf.'

'Just a leaf?'

The Witch laughed.

'I don't think it says a leaf,' she said.

Uncle Wizard frowned and re-read the spell.

*An A Leaf*

'What's an A-Leaf?'

'It comes from the A-Tree,' said The Witch.

Bob looked towards a nearby forest.

'Any around here?' he asked hopefully.

The Witch shook her head.

'There's only one A-Tree in the whole of the Land of Forever…'

'Where's that?' asked Uncle Wizard eagerly.

The Witch smiled.

'…at the centre of the Maze of Infinity.'

Bob tugged at his bobble hat thoughtfully.

'The Maze of Infinity…there's going to be monsters, isn't there?'

'Oh yes,' said The Witch. 'Lots!'

'Don't worry Bob, we'll be fine,' said Uncle Wizard.

'Of course we will,' said The Witch cheerfully, 'but first we've got a picnic to eat…well, we had a picnic to eat.'

Bob burped.

'Sorry.'

# 16

The ground spiralled away.  Uncle Wizard and Bob rode with The Witch on her broomstick, headed for the Maze of Infinity.

'Is it far?' asked Uncle Wizard.

The wind rushed through their hair.  They climbed higher and higher until they flew alongside rocket-birds, and could reach out and touch the custard-clouds which hung lazily in the sky.  The Witch's broomstick was so effortless as it glided on its way that Bob dozed off into a peaceful sleep.

'Not far,' said The Witch.  'First we have to cross the Silent Desert and then the Sapphire Ocean.  We'll reach the Maze of Infinity in no time.'

As they flew The Witch pointed out the wondrous sights of the Land of Forever.  There was the Great Floating River of Rumble-Canyon and the Ice-Trees of Chilly-Forest.  They smelt the pong-turnips of Aroma-Farm and chatted to a gang of flying adventure-penguins journeying to Mount Judder.

Suddenly they hit a patch of bumpy air and Uncle Wizard almost fell off the broomstick.

'It can get a little rough up here sometimes,' said The Witch, 'hold on to me tightly.'

Uncle Wizard wrapped his arms around The Witch and they sped on through the glorious sky.  As they flew Uncle Wizard told The Witch all about his life as a wizard.  He told her how he had dreamt of being a Great Wizard, but how his spells kept ending in disaster. Only last week he had accidentally turned his teapot into a superhero. Every time he went to make a cup of tea his teapot would cry '*Captain Teapot to the rescue!*' and then zoom off to save a tea-bag in distress.

The Witch listened to Uncle Wizard's stories and guided the broomstick on towards the shimmering heat of the Silent Desert.

At the back of the broomstick Bob was talking in his sleep.

'*Pie, pie, pie, pie, pie...*'

He was dreaming about the biggest custard pie in the world. It was ten-foot tall and had to be carried around in a wheel-barrow.

'Yaaaaww...grrggghh!'

Suddenly Bob awoke with a start. The back of his neck was fiery-hot. He rubbed it, but still it prickled. Sleepily he turned around and was so terrified he almost fell off the broomstick.

'Err, I think we've got a problem!'

The sky behind him sizzled with ghastly fire. It crackled and spat with a rainbow of angry colours. The Witch turned around. An anxious look crossed her face. Suddenly a swarm of hideous creatures burst out of the flaming sky.

'Ghoths!' she said in alarm.

Bob gulped.

'What...what are Ghoths?'

'They are Grim Wizard's evil servants.'

The Ghoths poured through the burning sky. Their jagged wings flapped as one. Huge slavering fangs jutted from their mouths and their eyes were cold and devil-green. With frightening speed they plunged after The Witch's broomstick.

'Can we outrun them?' asked Uncle Wizard.

The Witch shook her head.

'Maybe we could outrun one Ghoth, but not that many…there must be almost a hundred…'

The Ghoths wailed and howled. It was the most fearful sound. Desperately The Witch searched for somewhere to hide, but they were flying over the Silent Desert. There was only wave after wave of endless sand beneath them.

Suddenly her eyes lit up.

'I have an idea!' she exclaimed.

The Witch kicked her broomstick and it plunged towards the desert floor. The Ghoths surged after them, screeching and howling like devil-cats. Just then a flaming spear shot through the air and sizzled just over Bob's head.

'Erm, how's the escape plan coming along?' he asked nervously.

'Any moment now,' said The Witch.

'Only they've started throwing spears at me.'

Uncle Wizard nodded and pointed to a burning hole right through his magic hat.

'You think you've got problems!'

The sky was ablaze with flaming spears. The Witch lurched and swerved, desperately dodging the onslaught.

'Uncle Wizard! Mr Bob! Hold tight!' she said anxiously. 'This may get a little uncomfortable.'

The Ghoths were gaining on them. Down and down the broomstick dived, plunging towards the desert floor. Suddenly The Witch began to chant. The words of an ancient spell filled the air and two sparkling balls of magic appeared in her hands. She held them aloft, took a deep breath and then hurled them towards the desert floor.

There was a ferocious explosion. Great waves of sand shot into the air. Uncle Wizard and Bob coughed and spluttered and shielded their eyes.

Suddenly everything went dark. The blistering light from the twin suns of the Land of Forever disappeared. Bob cautiously opened an eye and peered ahead. The two balls of magic had blasted into the sand and were burrowing a tunnel deep beneath the Silent Desert. The Witch's broomstick had dived straight into the mouth of the tunnel.

'Nice escape,' said Bob.

The Witch shook her head and pointed behind them. The Ghoths had followed the broomstick into the tunnel and were still on their tail.

'Aah,' said Uncle Wizard.

'Oh dear,' said Bob.

'Excellent,' said The Witch.

Bob looked shocked.

'Excellent?' he exclaimed. 'Whose side are you on?'

The Witch smiled and drove her broomstick on through the tunnel of sand. The tunnel twisted this way and that as the two balls of magic burnt a hole deep beneath the desert. Behind them the Ghoths were gaining on them. Spears sliced through the air and the tunnel echoed to the sound of their dreadful screams. The Witch kicked her broomstick and bolted faster through the tunnel of sand. Suddenly, up ahead, the balls of magic split up. One went left, the other to the right. Now there were two tunnels.

'Cover your eyes, cover your mouths,' said The Witch. 'It's now or never…!'

# 17

The two tunnels lay up ahead. One veered left, the other right. With terrible screams and slavering mouths the Ghoths flew down the tunnel of sand, desperately lunging for The Witch's broomstick.

'We're done for!' cried Bob.

Suddenly The Witch's fingertips came alive with magical-fizzing sparkles. The air crackled and a thousand swarming colours spiralled through the tunnel like bionic-rainbows.

Then came the explosion.

A tidal wave of white light whipped through the tunnel. It raged and thrashed, and ripped great chunks of sand out of the tunnel walls. In a flash the explosion turned into a sandstorm and blasted straight into the faces of the Ghoths.

'Hold tight!' urged The Witch.

In the commotion The Witch kicked her broomstick and dived into the left hand tunnel. The Ghoths were utterly blinded. A billion grains of sand scratched their faces. They howled and screamed and did not have a hope of guessing which tunnel the broomstick had taken.

'They've gone the wrong way!'

With a look of joy on his face Uncle Wizard watched as the Ghoths flew down the right-hand tunnel.

'We've done it!' cried Bob.

They all breathed a sigh of relief as the wailing

cries of the Ghoths slowly faded to silence. Up ahead the glowing ball of magic still burrowed relentlessly through the sand. Suddenly it began to climb. The colour of the sand grew lighter and lighter until, with a flash of light, the broomstick burst through the surface of the desert and back into the dazzling sunshine.

'Wooohooooo!' cried Uncle Wizard.

'Yeeehaaaaa!' cried Bob.

The broomstick left the golden sand behind and shot off towards the horizon.

'Well,' said Bob, 'if this doesn't deserve a pie, I don't know what does.'

Uncle Wizard nodded.

'It could be deserving of double-pie.'

'Double-pie!' exclaimed Bob wide-eyed. 'Imagine that. Pie followed by more pie. It's the stuff of dreams!'

At the front of the broomstick The Witch had a look of concern on her face. She squinted back towards the desert and shook her head.

'It wont be long before the Ghoths escape,' she said. 'I don't think it's safe for us to be out in the open like this. We need somewhere to hide.'

Just then something glinted far off in the distance.

'What's that?' asked Uncle Wizard.

The Witch's eyes lit up.

'The Sapphire Ocean. I have an idea. Let's travel to the Maze of Infinity in style!'

They sped across the sky towards the glittering sea. The breezy air ruffled their hair and a tiny shadow of the broomstick slithered across the ground far below. As they flew a flock of fodder-dogs riding a giant air-turtle passed them by on their way to the Bone Jungle. The whoosh of the air-turtles wings almost sent Uncle Wizard's hat tumbling away into the Green Ravine below.

'Look,' said The Witch eagerly pointing into the distance, 'there's the harbour. I think we may just be in time.'

With a kick of her heels the broomstick began to descend. It gracefully swooped through the sky and then zipped along just above the ground like a skimming-bird hunting for bugs.

'Wow!' exclaimed Bob.

The harbour was full to bursting with bobbing boats. There were dinghies and dredgers, steamers and tugs. But one boat stood out like no other. It was magnificent. A giant luxury cruiser. It had three funnels, gleaming white cabins and was to be hauled through the water by a herd of giant sea-elephants.

'*The Sea Adventurer,*' said The Witch proudly, 'I hope you like it.'

'We're going on that?' asked Uncle Wizard in disbelief.

'Oh yes,' said The Witch, 'I think we deserve a little pampering and we'll be safely hidden away from those Ghoths.'

And with the gentlest landing they touched down on the harbour, right before the gang-plank leading up to *The Sea Adventurer*.

'Come on,' said The Witch eagerly, 'this way. The Maze of Infinity awaits…'

# 18

*The Sea Adventurer's* horn gave a loud blast and Uncle Wizard, Bob and The Witch hurried up the gangplank.

'Three tickets to the Maze of Infinity please,' said The Witch.

An attendant wearing a shiny blue uniform helped them onboard and showed them to their cabins.  With two long blasts of the horn the giant sea-elephants took up the strain, and *The Sea Adventurer* pulled slowly out of the port into the glistening waters beyond.

After settling in Uncle Wizard and Bob got ready for dinner and went on deck to watch the sunset.  It was beautiful beyond belief.  Fiery reds and blazing purples set the sky alight.  The twin-suns of the Land of Forever sunk towards the horizon and for the briefest moment the waters of the Sapphire Ocean became crystal clear.

'Wow,' said Bob, 'have you ever seen anything like that?'

Far below the lapping waves grew a city of enchanted coral.  It burst out of the ocean floor and curled through the waters with angelic grace.  It was every colour of the rainbow, yellows, reds and vibrant greens, but through them all there shone a sapphire blue which sparkled with a gasping brilliance.

Uncle Wizard shook his head.

'That's just incredible.'

Slowly the twin-suns slipped below the horizon and the colour of the Sapphire Ocean returned to its swirling greens and blues. With a contented sigh the passengers on board *The Sea Adventurer* left the setting suns and made their way towards the grand dining-room for dinner.

Uncle Wizard and Bob stood waiting for The Witch outside her cabin. Bob's stomach was rumbling.

'Does it really take this long for a witch to get ready?' asked Bob impatiently.

'Apparently so,' said Uncle Wizard with a sigh, 'I mean, it took her two hours just to decide which spell to use to make her dress.'

'But she's been in there for hours, what can she be doing?'

Uncle Wizard shrugged.

'The mind boggles.'

Just then the cabin door opened and out stepped The Witch. She wore a beautiful dress of flowing silk and shoes that shimmered like diamonds. Uncle Wizard gasped. He had never seen anyone look so beautiful.

'Good evening gentlemen,' said The Witch.

'Good evening,' said Uncle Wizard with a stutter.

'Is it time for pie?' asked Bob.

The Witch smiled.

'Now which one of you fine gentlemen is going to escort me to dinner?'

Uncle Wizard held out his arm, and looking as proud as could be he led The Witch into the dinning room of *The Sea Adventurer*.

'Wow!' said Bob.

The dining room was magnificent. Huge chandeliers hung from the ceiling and wonderful paintings covered the walls. Waiters and waitresses bustled about and all the passengers wore their finest clothes. A waiter led Uncle Wizard, Bob and The Witch to a table and passed them the menu.

Bob quickly studied the menu.

'Erm…I'll have everything please,' he said.

'Everything?' queried the waiter.

'Yes, everything…in a pie.'

The food was stunning, even Bob's Everything Pie. He sat in his chair and stared lovingly at the empty plate.

'Now that was a good pie.'

When the meal had finished a big brass band struck up and quickly the dance-floor was full of graceful swaying couples. Elegant ball gowns flowed through the air and shiny shoes tapped on the polished floor.

'Come on,' said The Witch to Uncle Wizard, 'lets dance.'

Uncle Wizard coughed and spluttered nervously.

'Erm, I don't dance.'

The Witch grabbed his hand and yanked him out of his seat.

'You do now.'

The Witch led Uncle Wizard into the middle of the dance floor. At first he felt rather awkward, but with a nudge here and a helping hand there he quickly loosened up. Very soon Uncle Wizard and The Witch were moving and swaying with the best of them.

Back at the table Bob called the waiter over.

'Yes Mr Pigeon?'

'Erm, any more of that Everything Pie?'

The waiter looked astonished.

'You want more pie?'

'Oh yes.'

'But Mr Pigeon, you will explode.'

Bob tapped his bulging belly.

'There's always room for a bit more pie!'

At the end of the night an exhausted Uncle Wizard escorted The Witch back to her cabin. Behind them waddled a rather full-up pigeon.

'Well thank you Uncle Wizard for a lovely night.'

Uncle Wizard bowed.

'And thank you Madam Witch.'

The Witch said goodnight to Bob and then slipped into her cabin and closed the door. Uncle Wizard was rooted to the spot. He just stared at the door, his eyes misty and his mouth wide open.

'Oh no,' said Bob with a groan, 'you've fallen completely in love with her, haven't you?'

But Uncle Wizard did not hear him. He just stared at the door and sighed.

# 19

The twin suns of the Land of Forever cast a golden light over the Sapphire Ocean. *The Sea Adventurer* had glided through the night and as morning came so did the first sight of land. Uncle Wizard and Bob stood on the deck with their mouths open. Before them, stretching as far as the eye could see, was the Maze of Infinity.

'Wow!' said Bob.

'Crikes!' exclaimed Uncle Wizard.

'Incredible, isn't it?' said The Witch.

Uncle Wizard was utterly speechless. He could only nod. The Maze of Infinity was beyond belief. It was a never-ending, ever-growing, colossal, gigantic, epic labyrinth of twists and turns. Its walls towered higher than skyscrapers. They burst into the sky and sat amongst the clouds. Bright glittering lights lit up the entrance and thousands of eager people queued to enter the most incredible maze ever built.

Bob stared at the enormity of the Maze of Infinity and tugged his bobble hat thoughtfully.

'And this A-Tree we're looking for, it's only to be found at the centre of the maze?'

The Witch smiled nervously.

'Well, let's hope so.'

'Erm, you don't seem too sure.'

'How can I be?' said The Witch with a gentle shrug. 'No one has ever reached the centre of the Maze of Infinity before.'

'What!' exclaimed Bob.

The Witch patted Bob on the head.

'Oh, don't worry, I'm sure we'll find it.'

With a final tug on the heavy ropes the giant sea-elephants guided *The Sea Adventurer* into Infinity Port. The gangplank was lowered and with an excited buzz the passengers began to disembark and head straight towards the Maze of Infinity.

Uncle Wizard, Bob and The Witch were the last to leave *The Sea Adventurer*. At the top of the gangplank The Witch paused.

'Remember, there could be Ghoths anywhere. We must be careful.'

A path led from Infinity Port to the maze. Heading towards the entrance were hundreds of people of all shapes and sizes. There were giraffe-men with enormous necks and octopus-ladies with eight arms carrying eight handbags. There was even a man made entirely of steam who wafted and drifted on the gentle breeze.

Suddenly Bob cried out in alarm. A look of utter horror splashed across his face. Desperately he gasped for breath.

'What is it?' asked The Witch urgently, 'are there Ghoths? Have we been followed?'

Bob frantically shook his head.

'Is it Grim Wizard? Is he here?' asked Uncle Wizard.

'No, no,' said Bob panting with fear, 'it's even worse than that. I've just realised, it's 9 o'clock in the morning and I haven't had breakfast. Quick, get me a pie before its all too late!'

Uncle Wizard and The Witch breathed a huge sigh of relief. A short distance from the entrance to the maze they ordered breakfast at a food stall and sat down at a table. Bob had double pie followed by more double pie. As they ate they watched the crowds swarm about the maze. Expectant chatter filled the air as the eager people passed under the huge archway and entered the never-ending vastness of the Maze of Infinity.

Something was bothering Uncle Wizard.

'Erm, how do people leave the maze?'

'Dearie me, you are a one, aren't you,' said the waitress who had come to collect their plates. 'No one ever leaves the Maze of Infinity. You go in, you don't come out. Look…'

The waitress pointed to the exit of the maze. Above it hung a rusty old counter which recorded the number of people to successfully escape from the Maze of Infinity. The counter read *zero*.

'Aah,' said Uncle Wizard.

'Oh dear,' said Bob.

The waitress shook her head.

'They're all looking for the centre of the maze. All looking for the A-Tree. I don't reckon it exists. There's no centre to that maze.'

Bob had a worried look on his face.

'So what happens to all the people?'

The waitress looked around secretively.

'I reckon they get eaten…by monsters!'

The waitress collected the plates and quickly left the table. Uncle Wizard and Bob were utterly silent.

'Now, now boys,' said The Witch, 'lets not get downhearted. I'm sure there's a centre to the maze and I'm sure we'll find the A-Tree there. Now, come on, lets get going.'

Uncle Wizard, Bob and The Witch left the table and approached the huge towering archway that was the entrance to the Maze of Infinity.

'Yes, yes,' said Uncle Wizard trying to reassure himself, 'I'm sure we'll do just fine. I mean, what could possibly go wrong?'

Bob peered into the mysterious depths of the Maze of Infinity.

'Everything,' he said simply.

# 20

'Wow!' exclaimed Bob.

'Crikes alive!' spluttered Uncle Wizard.

The Maze of Infinity was an incredible maze on the outside, but it was astounding on the inside. As Uncle Wizard and Bob stepped through the giant archway they could barely believe their eyes. It was a bustling, swarming criss-cross of paths, passageways and quite the most extraordinary walls.

'Erm, they're talking…' said Bob disbelievingly.

'What are?' asked Uncle Wizard.

'The walls…'

Uncle Wizard gasped. The walls of the Maze of Infinity were built from anything and everything. Stacked on top of each other, as high as the eye could see were rusty cars, vases and washing machines. There were benches and dolls houses, cricket bats and rocking horses, all jammed together. And everything spoke. Lampposts chin-wagged with cupboards. Egg-whisks nattered with garden sheds.

Over on the far wall a cheery radiator greeted all the new visitors.

'Welcome, welcome and a very good morning,' it chirped with a sparklingly happy voice. 'Give yourself a cheer, you're standing in the greatest maze ever built. This is the Maze of Infinity. Will you find the centre? Will you find the exit? Good luck, I'm sure you'll make it…'

Just then Uncle Wizard had a thought.

'Hang on, we could leave the maze just by walking back out of the entrance.'

The Witch tapped Uncle Wizard on the shoulder and pointed behind them.

'What entrance?' she asked.

Uncle Wizard spun round and gasped in astonishment. Where seconds before had stood the huge archway, now there was just a solid wall of shoes, loos and wonky didgeridoos.

'How can that be?'

'Look....'

People appeared in the maze as if from thin air. They too had walked through the archway, only to find it was now a solid wall.

'That's some incredible magic,' exclaimed Uncle Wizard in awe.

The Witch stared at the solid wall with narrowed eyes. There was a pensive look on her face.

'Yes, isn't it just. I wonder…'

But The Witch's thoughts were lost in the hustle and bustle as the crowds of people set off in search of the centre of the maze.

'Well,' said Uncle Wizard as the maze briefly quietened, 'I believe we have an A-Tree to find. Which way should we go?'

Bob stepped forward and puffed out his chest.

'Leave that to me,' he said importantly.

With a look of concentration on his face Bob stared in every direction. He looked at the criss-cross of paths, through archways, pathways and long sweeping curves, until he suddenly pointed in one particular direction.

'That way...we definitely want to go that way...'

Uncle Wizard looked puzzled.

'Are you sure the centre of the maze is that way?'

Bob shook his head.

'No, but I can smell pies...'

With an eager stride Bob set off along a twisting, winding path. For a moment Uncle Wizard and The Witch stared at each other, and then with a shrug of their shoulders followed Bob.

The path meandered this way and that. High above them the Maze of Infinity climbed forever upwards. Even at the highest points the walls still spoke to each other. It was a non-stop hubbub of chatter, chin-wagging and nattering.

After a long walk down the winding path Uncle Wizard, Bob and The Witch came to a series of archways, all leading off in different directions.

Uncle Wizard scratched his head.

'Which way now?'

Over on the wall a very enthusiastic sewing machine called out to them.

'Take the left path, that's the way you want to go. Definitely left. You'll be at the centre of the maze in no time. Keep going!'

Uncle Wizard thanked the sewing-machine and they set off once again. Deeper and deeper they journeyed into the maze. At every step objects in the walls called out encouragingly. A giant combine-harvester gave them three cheers, a brightly coloured dustbin clapped and a paddling pool sung them a cheery song. With an eager step Uncle Wizard, Bob and The Witch skipped along the path, certain that the centre of the maze would be just around the corner.

Now and then they came across other people journeying through the maze. They met a man with banana-hands and a three-legged wobble-woman.

'Good afternoon!'

Passing them in the opposite direction was a lava-man. Tiny flames leapt off his body.

'Looking for the way out?' asked Uncle Wizard.

'Oh no,' said the lava-man, 'I'm looking for the centre. A rather kind bookcase told me it was this way.'

Uncle Wizard looked a little surprised.

'But we've just come from that way. A sewing machine told us this was the way.'

The lava-man shook his head.

'No, no, no. You've got it all wrong. I've just come from that way. The centre is this way...'

And with that he purposefully strode off into the distance.

'What's going on?' asked Bob uncertainly.

The Witch stood silently for a moment. She looked about the maze, at its infinite stretches of never-ending pathways.

'I'm not sure, but we'll carry on this way.'

On and on they walked. The twin suns of the Land of Forever edged across the sky as the afternoon drew on. Jam jars, fishing-boats and creaky iron gates encouraged them on their way,

107

but there was never the slightest hint they were nearing the centre of the maze.

'Are you sure we're going in the right direction?' asked Uncle Wizard doubtfully.

The Witch was about to open her mouth when a nearby coffee-machine piped up.

'Of course you're going in the right direction. This way leads to the centre of the maze. You're doing really well. You'll find the A-Tree in no time.'

Suddenly, from the opposite wall, came a wheezing cough. The screen of an old and battered television flickered and spluttered.

'Don't listen!' exclaimed the television hysterically. 'Don't listen to them! The Maze of Infinity, it's a…it's a…'

The coffee-machine gasped.

'Don't say anything! You know they're watching. We'll all be punished…'

The television's screen flickered like a snow storm.

'I don't care. They've got to know the truth. The Maze of Infinity…'

Smoke began to pour out of the television. Its screen went fuzzy and its knobs and buttons began to rattle. Desperately the television tried to finish its sentence.

'…they're all…they're all in…'

Sparks blasted out of the television. Smoke blew everywhere. Suddenly, for the briefest second, a single word flashed up on the television's screen. The word was *Danger!*. The television then exploded in a ball of flame.

Uncle Wizard gasped. He spun round and faced the coffee-machine. His voice was urgent.

'What was all that about. What's going on?'

The coffee machine seemed to shrink and squirm.

'Oh, you don't want to listen to that old television,' it said nervously. 'It was mad, utterly mad. The Maze of Infinity is a wonderful, wonderful place.'

'But you said *they're watching*. Who's watching?'

'I didn't say anything of the sort!' protested the coffee-machine indignantly. 'How dare you say that? Who could possibly be watching? No one's watching…no one at all…'

The Witch took a deep breath. There was an anxious look on her face.

'Come on,' she said, 'we should get moving.'

'But what's happening?' asked Uncle Wizard.

The Witch shook her head.

'All I know is that we should be careful.'

Cautiously they carried on their journey. The Maze of Infinity stretched off in every direction. Sometimes it was dead-straight with sharp angled turns, sometimes it swept along in mighty curves. Feeling thirsty Uncle Wizard found a sink in the wall and they drank fresh water from the tap. Bob found a pie-machine nestled in another wall and gorged himself on pie after delicious pie.

'Well, this seems like a good spot.'

Evening was drawing in and they stopped for the night in a cosy little alcove. Bob snuggled up on a blanket and instantly fell asleep. Uncle Wizard and The Witch sat and watched the sky change through a rainbow of colours as the twin-suns of the Land of Forever slipped out of view.

'Do you think there really is a centre to this maze?' asked Uncle Wizard.

The Witch was silent for a moment. As the suns disappeared the air got chilly and The Witch shivered. Uncle Wizard snuggled up close and put an arm round her shoulders.

'I'm sure it does,' said The Witch with a yawn, 'it has to. Grim Wizard must be stopped...and I'm sure you'll find the second part of the spell...'

Overhead the blues and reds of the sky gave way to a brilliant darkness and the bright twinkling of a billion stars. The Witch rested her head on Uncle Wizard's shoulders. Her eyes were sleepy.

'...but Uncle Wizard, it's the third part of the

spell I'm most worried about.'

And without another word The Witch drifted off to sleep.

# 21

It was a cold grey morning. Heavy black clouds hung in the sky and a light drizzle had begun to fall. Uncle Wizard, Bob and The Witch gathered up their things and set off on their way. They walked without speaking. Somehow it seemed a morning for silence.

The gloom had descended into the maze. A few objects in the wall cheered them along, but without the same sparkle as yesterday. A nervousness had gripped the Maze of Infinity.

Bob shook his head.

'I don't like this one bit.'

They carried on along the path. The maze turned at sharp angles and they ducked through shadowy archways. Now and then they would see other people shuffling along in the gloom, but barely a word was spoken as they passed.

Suddenly a crack of lightning ripped through the sky. The clouds flashed and flared with venomous colour. Heavy rain began to fall.

'We need to find somewhere to shelter,' said The Witch.

Puddles began to form on the ground. Streams trickled between the walls. Uncle Wizard, Bob and The Witch hurried through the maze before they came across a huge archway and sheltered from the rain.

Uncle Wizard wiped the drips from his face.

'I guess we'll just have to wait here.'

The Witch looked worried. On the other side of the archway a large clearing opened out. The rain made it look misty and pale. A few thorny shrubs poked out of the ground, but otherwise it was barren and lifeless. On the far side of the clearing a small archway stood in the wall.

'We can't stay here,' said The Witch firmly.

'Why not?' asked Uncle Wizard.

The Witch looked to the sky. It churned and curdled with ominous intent.

'Something's not right. Something's happening. We have to get moving.'

Another crack of lightning ripped across the sky. Booming thunder shook the ground.

The Witch turned urgently to Uncle Wizard.

'We're going to cross the clearing. We're going to head for the archway on the other side…'

She paused for a moment and took a deep breath.

'…if anything should happen, I want you to promise me you'll go on. I want you to promise me you'll complete the spell. No matter how dangerous, no matter how difficult, you must promise me you wont give up?'

Uncle Wizard was taken aback.

'But you're coming with us, aren't you?'

The Witch looked towards the thunderous sky.

'I hope so, but please, you must promise me?'

'I promise,' said Uncle Wizard solemnly.

'Thank you,' said The Witch.

Urgently she led them out into the clearing. A cold wind whipped into their faces and the rain pounded down fiercely. They headed straight for the far archway, never daring to slow their pace for an instant.

Another flash of lightning lit up the sky. A great rumble came from the clouds. It seemed as if the sky would crack open.

They were halfway across the clearing. The archway on the far side was getting nearer. Their feet splashed through puddles and their breath filled the air. Every gust of wind tried to knock them back, but on and on they struggled.

'Oh my!'

Suddenly The Witch gasped. A look of utter panic covered her face. The sky had crumbled. The clouds boiled violent red.

'Run!' she screamed, 'run, now!'

Uncle Wizard was startled.

'What?'

'Just run!' screamed The Witch.

after wave of jagged lightning-bolts blasted through the sky.

'YOU WILL BE DESTROYED!'

The Witch swerved violently. Her broomstick dived towards the ground as she desperately tried to avoid Grim Wizard's evil magic.

Uncle Wizard and Bob held their breath. They stood by the edge of the clearing and watched helplessly as The Witch plummeted towards the ground.

'Pull up! Pull up!' cried Uncle Wizard.

The bolts of devil-light screamed through the sky. In seconds the broomstick would be turned to fire and ash. Suddenly The Witch performed a dizzying loop-the-loop. She flipped through the sky and came right up behind the devil-light.

'I will not let you win this time, Grim Wizard!'

Her hands twinkled. A spell was whispered on

her lips. There was a flash of magic and the jagged bolts of lightning simply stopped. They froze in mid-air and then like glistening snow, fell gently to the ground.

Grim Wizard howled with rage.

'NOW YOU WILL FEEL MY TRUE POWER...'

But The Witch was too quick for him. She shot through the sky like a speeding arrow and blasted Grim Wizard with a shower of sparkling magic from the bristles of her broomstick. Grim Wizard caught the full blast. He tumbled through the sky and cried out in pain.

'She's doing it!' exclaimed Uncle Wizard, 'she's going to defeat Grim Wizard!'

Bob tugged at his bobble hat anxiously.

'But I thought only a wizard could defeat Grim Wizard...'

Suddenly the sky turned dreadfully dark. Grim Wizard's cry of pain turned into a howl of booming laughter. He snuffed out The Witch's magic with a wave of his hand and hung fearlessly amongst the swirling, nightmare colours of the sky.

'YOU ARE MORE FOOLISH THAN YOUR SISTERS. NO WITCH CAN DEFEAT ME!'

Grim Wizard raised his hands. He let out a blood-curdling cry and then launched a devastating attack.

Devil-light sliced through the sky. The Witch tried to dodge and weave, but even she could not escape. First one blast caught her, then another. Grim Wizard howled with laughter and sent another blistering attack towards the defenceless witch.

There was nothing she could do. The devil-light crashed into her like a tidal-wave and she slumped unconscious on her broomstick.

Grim Wizard roared in victory.

'I AM INVINCIBLE!'

He soared down and grabbed the slumped body of The Witch. With a merciless cry he kicked away her broomstick and sent it hurtling into the raging clouds and far over the horizon. He then hung in the air with The Witch draped over his arm like a rag-doll. A booming laugh curdled the air and then he stared menacingly down at Uncle Wizard.

'I WILL RETURN FOR YOU.'

With untold power Grim Wizard opened a hole in the sky. Uncle Wizard cried out in desperation, but Grim Wizard headed straight for the hole. In utter panic Uncle Wizard rifled through his pockets for a spell, any spell. He must do something to save The Witch. But it was too late. All he could do was watch helplessly as Grim Wizard flew into the darkness of the hole and disappeared. The last thing he saw before the hole closed up was a single tear drip from The Witch's eye.

'She's gone...'

Uncle Wizard slumped to the floor, utterly drained. He felt cold and lifeless, as if his heart had been wrenched from his body. The Witch was gone, taken by Grim Wizard. How could he go on?

'Bob, what am I going to do?'

Bob was unusually silent. He stood staring into the sky with a curious look on his face.

'I think you should have a look at this...'

Uncle Wizard struggled to his feet. His cloak was crumpled and his hat was bent. With tired, hopeless eyes he looked towards the sky.

'What is it?'

His heart began to flutter. A touch of colour returned to his cheeks. Falling through the sky was a golden droplet.

'It's The Witch's tear,' said Bob, 'I saw it fall from her eye.'

The tear plummeted towards the ground. It sparkled like a brilliant diamond and lit up the clearing. Uncle Wizard and Bob were transfixed. It was so beautiful, so small and perfect they could not take their eyes from it. With a splash it landed in a puddle by their feet.

Uncle Wizard held his breath.

Suddenly the puddle erupted in a shower of wondrous light. It blossomed into the air, and there, stood before them, was a vision of The Witch. She was made of light, but fading fast.

*'You promised me Uncle Wizard, you promised me you'd save the world…'*

Uncle Wizard was stunned. He stared at the wispy figure before him with his mouth wide open.

*'You must go on, Uncle Wizard, you must defeat Grim Wizard.'*

The Witch faded fast. With the very last ray of light she looked straight at Uncle Wizard and smiled a smile of such tenderness and hope it made Uncle Wizard dance with joy.

'She knows I can do it. She believes in me!'

His face lit up like a summer's day. He jumped onto a boulder, threw up his arms and bellowed at the top of his voice.

'My name is Uncle Wizard. I'm going to save the world!'

# 23

The twin suns of the Land of Forever blazed down upon the Maze of Infinity. Crisp shadows criss-crossed the pathways, and from the towering walls came the sound of excited chatter.

'This way!'

'You're nearly there!'

Uncle Wizard strode through the Maze of Infinity with a look of determination on his face. He turned left then right with such purposefulness it was as if he visited the centre of the maze everyday.

'Not long now, Bob,' he said confidently, 'we'll soon find the A-Tree.'

Bob was not so convinced. All the watering-cans and milk-floats nestled in the walls of the maze told them they were going the right way, but how could they be sure? They could wander for a hundred years and never get close to the centre of the maze. Plus there was a more important problem.

'Is it lunch-time yet?'

Uncle Wizard sighed.

'We had lunch ten minutes ago.'

'We did?' said Bob in surprise.

'Yes, you remember, you ate five pies.'

'I thought that was breakfast.'

'No, breakfast was when you ate ten pies.'

Bob tugged at his bobble hat thoughtfully. It seemed a lot longer than ten minutes since he had eaten a pie.  Suddenly he was filled with hope.

'Is it time for Lunch 2?'

Uncle Wizard groaned.

'There's no such thing as Lunch 2.  And anyway we're all out of pies.  You've eaten the lot.'

Bob gasped.

'No more pies!  This is a disaster.'

Uncle Wizard smiled.

'Of course, I could always make you a pie with a spell?'

Bob looked aghast.

'Erm, err, well, you know, I think I'll pass.  I'm not really that hungry anymore.'

The last time Uncle Wizard attempted to make pies out of magic had been a complete disaster.  His pies had looked like pies, they had even smelt like pies, unfortunately they had not behaved like pies.  Instead of sitting on a plate waiting to be eaten, the pies had started sneezing.  No matter how hungry Bob was, no matter how much he loved pies, he was never going to eat a pie that sneezed.

Without another word about pies they carried on through the Maze of Infinity.  For long stretches they walked in silence.  Uncle Wizard thought about The Witch.  Not only did he have to save the world, he also had to save her.  But there was something bothering him.

'Just before she was captured The Witch said she was most worried about the third part of the spell.'

Bob tugged thoughtfully at his bobble hat.

'What is the third part?'

Uncle Wizard shrugged and then reached inside his magic cloak and pulled out the spell. Carefully he unrolled the scroll.

'Now, what have we here?'

Uncle Wizard read the spell. The three parts were listed in order. First came the Tooth of a Thunder Troll. As Uncle Wizard read he proudly stroked the tooth nestled in his pocket. Next was an A-Leaf. Surely they would soon find the centre of the Maze of Infinity. Finally, its letters still jumbled, was the final part of the spell:

*TWI CHETH FO TRA HEETH*

As he read the words Uncle Wizard shivered. It was as if his blood had turned to ice. He had no idea what the third part was, but there was something worrying about it.

Bob read the words and gasped.

'What is it?' asked Uncle Wizard. 'Have you worked out what the third part of the spell is?'

Bob shook his head, but his heart was beating fast. The third part of the spell was something terrible, he just knew it.

'I don't know,' he said quietly, 'but I don't think we can worry about it when we've still got the centre of the maze to find.'

Just then a sewing-machine called out to them.

'Well, maybe I can help. If you're looking for the centre of the maze?' said the sewing machine cheerfully. 'Why not take the bus?'

'Bus?' exclaimed Uncle Wizard in surprise.

'Oh yes, the bus,' said the sewing-machine, 'the bus to the centre of the maze. And of course, you'll want to know where the bus-stop is, and my, what a bus-stop it is. You'll hardly believe your eyes, or ears! Just follow the path round the corner and take the first left. You can't miss it. Any questions?'

'Just one,' said Bob.

'Yes?'

'Will there be any pies?'

# 24

It was astonishing. Uncle Wizard ducked under the archway and there, in the late afternoon sunshine was the most amazing sight in the whole of the Maze of Infinity.

'It's…it's incredible!' he spluttered. 'Quick Bob, come and see!'

Uncle Wizard pointed and waved like a madman. Bob followed him underneath the archway and stared. He squinted, shuffled his feet and then tugged at his bobble hat with a bemused look on his face.

'Isn't it wonderful!' exclaimed Uncle Wizard.

'No,' said Bob, 'it's just a bus-stop.'

'Oh,' cried Uncle Wizard joyously, 'but it's so much more than that. This is the bus-stop, the wondrous bus-stop to the centre of the Maze of Infinity!'

Bob shrugged his shoulders.

'I'm more of a pie man…'

Before them, in the middle of a square lined with flowers, was a bus-stop beyond imagination. It was a bus-stop made of music. So enchanting, so vibrant was the music it could actually be seen. The music twinkled out of the ground and formed the shape of the most incredible bus-stop, eyes had ever seen.

Hundreds of people surrounded the bus-stop. They stared with mesmerised eyes and listened with enchanted ears. More and more people were drawn into the square. They came through the archways with their faces full of joy. Soon a thousand people stood listening to the enchanting sounds.

'It's so beautiful,' said Uncle Wizard, utterly enraptured.

Bob stared at him in disbelief.

'You're behaving really weird,' he said with a shake of his head. 'Not even Weird Wizard is this weird, and his best friend is a turnip…'

Suddenly the music changed. The crowd gasped as the bus-stop showered out music like a glittering waterfall. Droplets of song fell on the people like summer rain and made them dance and sing with joy.

'I've never felt so happy,' said Uncle Wizard. 'I could stay here forever and ever.'

Bob gasped.

'But what about The Witch! What about saving the world?'

Uncle Wizard waved the question away.

'Oh, that can wait,' he said dreamily. 'I just want to listen to the music. The beautiful, beautiful music...'

Bob was worried. Something was wrong. He tugged on Uncle Wizard's magic-cloak, but as he did so there came the most magnificent sound of a trumpet. All the people gasped and turned towards the grand entrance to the square.

The buses were arriving!

One by one they came. A fleet of blazing red double-decker buses. The people cried with joy.

'Look! The buses...they're flying!'

The buses did not have wheels. Where the wheels should have been were huge powerful wings. They beat gently in the air and carried the buses a few feet off the ground. Like ballet dancers the buses swept into the square and lined up at the bus-stop made of music.

'Isn't this incredible!' cried Uncle Wizard in delight.

Bob narrowed his eyes and shook his head.

'This is a trap...'

Uncle Wizard's eyes were glazed and dreamy.

'Is it? That's nice...'

The doors of the buses whooshed open and

out stepped smartly dressed bus attendants.

'Good evening ladies and gentlemen,' said one of the attendants, 'welcome to the tour to the centre of the Maze of Infinity. I hope you enjoy your trip. Please board your allotted bus and take your seat.'

Bob was frantic. He watched in dismay as the crowds of people climbed onto the buses. Their eyes were misty and far away. He tugged urgently on Uncle Wizard's cloak.

'We can't do this. We can't get on board...'

'Nonsense, nonsense,' said Uncle Wizard dreamily. 'Come on, it's our turn...'

'Don't get on!' cried Bob.

He desperately grabbed Uncle Wizard's cloak, but Uncle Wizard leapt through the open door, dragging Bob with him. With a whoosh the bus doors closed behind them.

Bob gulped.

'We're doomed!'

An attendant led them up to the top deck and to two empty seats right at the front. Outside the last of the people clambered onboard the amazing flying buses. Finally the square emptied and the buses all rang their bells.

'Please fasten your seatbelts,' said the bus driver over the loudspeaker, 'we are ready to depart.'

With the smoothest, most graceful of movements the fleet of buses beat their wings and glided out of the square. It was an incredible sight. A hundred double-decker buses all packed with people, all flying in line like a flock of migrating birds.

Uncle Wizard stared out of the window.

'I've never been happier,' he said joyously. 'We're off to…to…oh, it doesn't matter where we're going. Who cares about anything…'

Bob was terrified. Uncle Wizard had forgotten about The Witch, and forgotten about saving the world. Now he could not even remember where the bus was going.

The buses flew on through the Maze of Infinity. Their wings beat against the air as they glided along the pathways. The objects in the walls shouted encouragement. All the passengers waved back eagerly. Slowly the buses began to climb. They rose higher and higher, leaving the ground far below.

Bob looked despairingly out of the window.

'We need to get off this bus,' he pleaded, 'I don't think we're even going to the centre of the maze.'

'I know, isn't it wonderful,' said Uncle Wizard.

Bob was shocked.

'Can't you understand anything I say?'

'Of course I can Susan. We'll go swimming with the penguins after lunch.'

Bob gasped. Uncle Wizard had lost his mind. He looked around. All the other passengers were the same. Some of them had big stupid grins on their faces, some just gazed dreamily at nothing at all. It must have been the bus-stop. Somehow they had all been hypnotised by the bus stop's music.

The fleet of sparkling red buses climbed higher and higher. The twin suns of the Land of Forever had disappeared over the horizon and now the sky twinkled with a billion stars. Bob looked desperately out of the window. Soon they would climb above the towering walls and leave the maze entirely.

'We're doomed!'

The bus soon echoed to the sound of snoring. Bob turned around. All the passengers were fast asleep, their heads nestled in soft cushions.

'Come on,' said Bob to Uncle Wizard, 'we've got to escape. We've got to get off this bus.'

But like the other passengers Uncle Wizard was sound asleep. Bob tried to wake him, but no matter how hard he shook him, nothing worked.

'Wake up! Wake up!' he pleaded.

'Is anything the matter?'

Silently one of the bus attendants had crept up behind Bob. She wore a sparkling uniform and smiled brightly. Bob gulped. There was something terribly worrying about the attendants. He had to be careful. He could trust no one.

'Erm, no, no, everything's fine,' he said nervously. 'Just trying to wake my friend.'

The attendant smiled.

'Oh, but he looks so peaceful, best to let him sleep. Why don't you get some rest yourself?'

'Oh, I'm not tired,' replied Bob.

'Well, would you like something to eat then? A delicious pie perhaps?'

Bob's eyes lit up. A delicious pie! Perhaps these attendants were not so bad after all. The attendant passed Bob a pie and with barely a pause he took a giant bite.

'Sweet dreams,' said the attendant with a smile.

Bob looked puzzled. Why had the attendant said that? But after a single mouthful he suddenly found he was incredibly sleepy. The pie! There had been something in the pie to send him to sleep.

'We're doomed!'

Bob's head swayed this way and that. He could barely keep his eyes open. He had to wake Uncle Wizard. It was their only hope. He groggily reached inside Uncle Wizard's pocket and dragged out the bottle of whiz-bang powder. Whenever Uncle Wizard had too much Wizard-Juice he always woke himself up with a dash of whiz-bang powder.

Bob only hoped it would work now.

Clumsily he removed the top. Barely managing to stay awake he poured a dash into Uncle Wizard's mouth. He screwed the top back on, yawned like he had never yawned before and then fell into a deep, dark sleep.

With his last thought Bob desperately hoped Uncle Wizard would wake up. Otherwise their wonderful adventure was over...

# 25

The flying buses soared high into the dark night-sky. With each powerful beat of their wings the towering walls of the Maze of Infinity dwindled away to become mere specks on the ground. The attendants on Uncle Wizard's bus smiled. All was as it should be.

'Every passenger is asleep,' said an attendant reporting back.

'Good,' said the chief attendant. 'Make sure none of them wake-up…ever!'

The attendants laughed and the fleet of buses flew on. Not a single bus headed for the centre of the maze. Not a single passenger knew they had been tricked. Slumped in their seats they were all fast asleep…

All except one.

'Crikes!'

From the top deck came a spluttering cry. A drop of whiz-bang powder trickled down Uncle Wizard's throat and he awoke with a start. He shuddered, shivered, and looked utterly confused.

'Err, where am I?'

With uncertain eyes he took in his surroundings. He was sitting on a bus. How had he ended up on a bus?

'And what's this funny taste in my mouth?' he asked himself groggily. 'What's going on?'

He scratched his head, he waggled a finger in his ear and then noticed something rather alarming.

The bus was not attached to the ground.

'Good grief, it's a flying bus!'

Uncle Wizard was utterly baffled. The last thing he remembered was talking to a sewing machine about a bus-stop. After that everything was a blank.

'Bob?'

Bob was slumped on the seat next to him.

'Bob…Bob?'

No matter how hard Uncle Wizard shook Bob he could not wake him up. Then he noticed the bottle of whiz-bang powder. That was the funny taste in his mouth! He rubbed his eyes and looked out of the window. The stars shone brightly and the moon twinkled in the midnight sky. There was no sign of the Maze of Infinity.

Something was wrong.

'What are you doing, you shouldn't be awake!'

An attendant had heard Uncle Wizard's cry and rushed up the stairs to the top-deck. She spoke with a gruff voice.

'Stay there, I'll get something to make you sleep.'

Uncle Wizard gulped. There was something alarming about the attendant. Her eyes were cold and her voice was angry. Uncle Wizard felt as if he were a prisoner rather than a passenger.

As the attendant marched away Uncle Wizard noticed another bus flying close by. All its passengers were fast asleep, exactly like those on this bus. What was going on? Where were they being taken? For a moment he was lost in thought and then, as the other bus flew very close by, Uncle Wizard saw something utterly terrifying.

He almost screamed.

'Ghoths!'

There were Ghoths on the other bus. Grim Wizard's evil assistants had taken it over. Uncle Wizard was just about to run and tell the attendants when suddenly it dawned on him, the attendants were in disguise. The attendants were Ghoths!.

His heart sank. They were in the gravest danger. From the lower deck he heard gruesome voices. The Ghoths' had taken off their disguises. They would be coming for him at any moment.

'We have to get off this bus!'

Uncle Wizard pulled out his spell book and flicked from page to page, desperately looking for a parachute spell. He then rifled through his magic-cloak and pulled out his potions and powders.

From below came the voice of a Ghoth.

'Tell the master, we have the wizard.'

Uncle Wizard gasped. This spell had to work. Into his hat he threw dollops of ooze-juice and slithers of slap-shadow. In went zoink-dust, puff-wind and zoom-bubbles. Quickly he mixed the spell. Hunched over his magic hat, with bursting light filling the bus, he added a drop of whiz-bang powder.

The magic-hat exploded with colour. Smoke and flames flashed through the bus. Uncle Wizard wafted away the smoke and gasped.

'Good grief!' he exclaimed in amazement.

The spell had worked! There on the floor was

a parachute. Uncle Wizard strapped it on, then grabbed Bob and ran to the back of the bus.

At the sound of the explosion the Ghoths charged up the stairs.

'Find the wizard!'

'He must not escape!'

Uncle Wizard hid at the back of the bus as the Ghoths disappeared into the smoke at the front. For a split second the coast was clear. Uncle Wizard raced for the stairs.

The Ghoths were blinded by the smoke, but quickly discovered that Uncle Wizard was missing.

'Find him!'

'Get him!'

Uncle Wizard jumped down the stairs and landed with a clatter on the lower deck. Right before him were the double doors. Without a thought he yanked the emergency handle and the doors sprang open. An icy blast of air hit him in the face.

Angry cries came from the top deck. The Ghoths hurtled down the stairs.

Uncle Wizard stood at the very edge of the doors. A gushing wind whipped his cloak and the cold air froze his bones. Below, the night sky looked ominous.

The Ghoths reached the bottom of the stairs.

'There, get him!'

Uncle Wizard took a deep breath. He closed his eyes, and with Bob in his pocket and his parachute on his back he jumped out of the flying bus and into the dark night sky.

# 26

'Err, what's happening?'

Bob stuck his head outside Uncle Wizard's pocket. He yawned, wiped the sleep from his eyes, and then suddenly realised that something was very, very wrong.

Uncle Wizard patted him on the head.

'Nothing to worry about,' he said cheerily, 'I've got everything under control.'

This did not reassure Bob in the slightest.

'Something's not right…something's missing. What's going on?'

Uncle Wizard took a deep breath.

'Well, where do I start?' he said excitedly. 'There I was sitting on a bus…not any old bus mind you, but a flying bus. Imagine that! No idea how I ended up there, I can't remember a thing. Well, anyway it turns out we'd been kidnapped by Ghoths! But don't worry, we've escaped from the bus.'

Bob was a little hesitant.

'How did we escape?'

Uncle Wizard smiled widely.

'Simple really! Jumped straight out of the main doors. Those Ghoths didn't see that coming!'

Bob suddenly became very worried about the something that was missing.

'Erm, just one question…'

'Yes?'

'Where's the ground?'

Uncle Wizard took a deep breath.

'Well, there's a thing,' said Uncle Wizard reassuringly. 'Now, as you may be aware the thing about flying buses is that they fly...and they tend to fly above the ground...quite high above the ground as it turns out...'

Bob looked around. Everything was dark. The only sound was a squealing rush of wind.

'Now,' continued Uncle Wizard, 'if you look down there, can you see that large thing with all the lights?'

Bob looked down, a long way down.

'What, that large thing with all the lights hurtling towards us really fast?'

'That's the fellow...well, that's the ground...'

Suddenly Bob came to his senses. Uncle Wizard had jumped out of the flying bus. They were falling through the sky!

'Aaaaaaaaaaaaaaaarrrghhhhhhhh!!!!'

Uncle Wizard let Bob have a good scream.

'Now, don't worry, Bob,' he said tapping the bulging package on his back. 'I've got a parachute.'

'Where did you get a parachute from?'

'I made it...with a spell!'

'Aaaaaaaaaaaaaaaarrrghhhhhhhh!!!!'

Uncle Wizard and Bob hurtled through the dark night sky. The air was freezing and the wind was vicious. Down below, the ground rushed towards them.

'We're doomed!' cried Bob.

Uncle Wizard shook his head.

'Nonsense, we'll be fine. All I need to do is pull

this handle and we'll float to the ground using this fine parachute.'

'Pull it, then!' pleaded Bob. 'Pull it!'

'All in good time,' said Uncle Wizard calmly. 'Now, this is nice, isn't it? Just tumbling through the sky.'

'Pull the handle,' screamed Bob. 'Pull it now!'

'Oh, very well then.'

Uncle Wizard took hold of the handle. Both his and Bob's eyes were fixed on the parachute. With a hard tug, Uncle Wizard pulled the handle. The parachute opened. A hundred lines of string burst out.

Something was wrong…

'Aah,' said Uncle Wizard.

'Oh dear,' said Bob.

The spell had been a disaster. There was no parachute!

Uncle Wizard and Bob looked in utter dismay as the lines of string burst out of the bag. Instead of a parachute, attached to each line of string was a potato. Not any old potato, these were dapper potatoes. Potatoes dressed in bow-ties and the finest suits. And just as matters could not get any worse for Uncle Wizard and Bob, the potatoes began to sing…

*'Mash me, roast me, boil me, mate-eo,*
*Here I am, a singing potato,*
*Round and brown and lovely with gravy,*
*Don't eat me? You must be crazy.'*

*Peel me, jacket me, chip me, mate-eo,*
*Can you believe I'm a singing potato,*
*Put me in the oven, put me on a plate,*
*I'm a singing potato, aren't I great?*

Uncle Wizard looked at Bob.  Bob looked at Uncle Wizard.  They both screamed.

'Aaaaaaaaaaaaaaarrrghhhhhhh!!!!'

Down and down they fell, tumbling head over heels through the sky.  The ground rushed towards them.  The lights got larger and brighter.

142

'We're doomed!' cried Bob again.

'Don't worry,' said Uncle Wizard, 'there is a plan B...'

'What's plan B?' asked Bob desperately.

Uncle Wizard opened his mouth, took the deepest breath, and then bellowed at the top of his voice.

'HELP!!!!!!!!!'

And as they plummeted like stones, Uncle Wizard's voice carried to the farthest reaches of the Land of Forever. It carried beyond the Gangle Mountains, over the Iron Sea, and across the Fields of Fire, until finally, desperately, Uncle Wizard's cry for help was heard...

Suddenly there was a flash of light on the horizon. Like a shooting star a fiery spear raced across the dark night sky. It rocketed over the Musty Jungle and zoomed by the Idle Waterfall. One end was made from the smoothest wood, at the other end sat springy and sparkling bristles.

'The Witch's broomstick!' cried Uncle Wizard. 'We're saved.'

The Witch's broomstick dived through the sky towards them. The ground was just seconds away. It swooped underneath Uncle Wizard and Bob and with a shudder and a bounce caught them perfectly. They glided gently away from the ground.

'That was a close one,' said Uncle Wizard.

Bob shook his head.

'Plan B was the worst plan ever!'

Uncle Wizard smiled.

'Just be glad we didn't try plan C...'

The broomstick whooshed over the ground and as their eyes adjusted to the light, Uncle Wizard and Bob realised they were back in the Maze of Infinity. The broomstick landed and they found themselves in the middle of a clearing. It was so dark that neither of them could see a thing. Without warning the broomstick shot off and disappeared into the sky.

'Well,' said Uncle Wizard, 'perhaps we should get some sleep. We still have an A-Tree to find. It could be a long day tomorrow.'

Uncle Wizard and Bob found a soft patch of ground and almost immediately they both fell asleep.

Bob dreamt about pies.

Uncle Wizard dreamt about The Witch.

# 27

Uncle Wizard snored. With every snore his fluffy beard rose, wriggled in the wind and then settled back down on his chin. He made quite a racket.

'Sshh,' said an ironing board.

'Quiet!' said a piano.

The twin suns had risen over the Land of Forever and the Maze of Infinity twinkled in the glorious morning sunshine.

Uncle Wizard kept snoring.

'Button it,' said a scooter.

'Hush,' said a trampoline.

In the huge towering wall above where Uncle Wizard slept, a rusty old rake had had enough. With a flick of its handle it pinged a pebble at the snoring wizard. The pebble bounced off his stomach and twanged him on his nose.

'Crikes!' cried Uncle Wizard as he was startled awake.

After an enormous yawn Uncle Wizard struggled to his feet and stretched out his arms and legs. Bob still dozed and the walls settled back down to sleep. Uncle Wizard carefully tiptoed backwards across the clearing and then slowly, without making a sound, he turned around.

'Waaaahhhhhhaaaaaahhh!'

Uncle Wizard screamed. His lungs bellowed louder than a thousand fog horns. The whole of the clearing was awake in an instant. Bob leapt up and flapped around in a panic.

'What...who...why?'

Across the clearing, in the hazy mist of early morning, Uncle Wizard leapt around like a kangaroo on a pogo-stick. He waved his arms and shouted for joy.

'It's here! It's here!'

Bob looked bewildered. He waddled across the clearing and stood next to Uncle Wizard. Suddenly his jaw dropped open in utter astonishment.

'Is that...'

'Yes! Yes!' screamed Uncle Wizard. 'We've done it! We've done it! We've reached the centre of the Maze of Infinity...we've found the A-Tree!!!'

Right before Bob's eyes was the A-Tree. It stood tall and proud in the centre of the clearing. It was the most magnificent tree Bob had ever seen.

'The Witch's broomstick,' cried Uncle Wizard. 'It took us to the centre of the maze. We've been sleeping next to the A-Tree all night long!'

The A-Tree was in the shape of a perfect letter 'A'. Its leaves were velvety and soft. Its bark was smooth and strong. Uncle Wizard and Bob stared at it, half in amazement, half in disbelief.

'So,' said Bob eventually, 'this is it. We just take a leaf and we're off?'

Uncle Wizard shrugged.

'I guess so.'

Uncle Wizard walked up to the A-Tree, took a deep breath and then reached out a hand to pluck off a leaf.

*Thwack!*

The A-Tree whacked him across the hand with a branch.

'Ouch!' cried Uncle Wizard in pain.

The A-Tree rustled its leaves and stood still.

Bob shook his head.

'Leave this to me,' he said.

Bob waddled up to the A-Tree and reached out a wing.

*Thwack!*

The A-Tree whacked him across the beak.

'Ouch!' cried Bob.

Over on the far wall a dented dustbin beckoned to Uncle Wizard and Bob. The dustbin tutted and sighed.

'No, no, no,' it said knowledgeably. 'If you want a leaf from the A-Tree you need to creep up on it, catch it unawares.'

Uncle Wizard and Bob nodded and then casually crept across the clearing towards the A-Tree. They pretended to chat about the weather. They even whistled a jaunty song. They crept right up beside the tree, pretended to walk past, and then just at the last second Uncle Wizard flicked out a hand.

'What...where's it gone?'

Uncle Wizard's hand grasped thin air. The A-Tree had jumped up and fled across the other side of the clearing. Uncle Wizard stared for a moment in disbelief. He stroked his beard thoughtfully and then smiled, tapped his nose and gave Bob a knowing wink.

'Well Bob, I can't hang around here any longer,' he exclaimed theatrically, 'its time for my turnip-juggling lesson. Goodbye!'

Uncle Wizard turned and began to walk towards the exit archway. He scratched his ear, swatted away a fly and then suddenly, with lightning speed, twisted around and with one mighty leap threw himself at the A-Tree.

*Splat!*

Uncle Wizard fell flat on his face. Bob tugged at his bobble hat nervously.

'Erm, I think you might want to look at this.'

Uncle Wizard rubbed his eyes and looked up. The A-Tree had fled. It ran as fast as it could towards the archway, its leaves rustling, its branches twanging. Uncle Wizard leapt to his feet. He stood in the middle of the clearing and pointed towards the archway.

'Quick Bob,' he cried, 'follow that tree!'

The chase was on! Without a moment to lose Uncle Wizard and Bob were after the A-Tree. They raced across the clearing and headed for the exit.

'Left, left,' cried Bob, 'it's turning left!'

The A-Tree reached the archway and hurtled off along one of the long sweeping paths of the Maze of Infinity.

'Come on,' said Uncle Wizard, 'we can't let it get away.'

The A-Tree kicked up dust as it raced through the maze. It ducked beneath arches, hurtled through clearings and raced round corners. Bob wheezed and spluttered. He was not sure how long he could keep this up.

'It's getting away,' he sighed.

'Come on, no slacking,' said Uncle Wizard. 'There'll be triple pie for whoever catches the A-Tree.'

'Triple pie!' exclaimed Bob.

Suddenly, like a mega-boom rocket, Bob launched himself after the A-Tree. His little legs thundered across the ground and his eyes burned with fiery determination. Very soon they were catching the A-Tree.

'Right, right, it's turning right.'

Bob ran round the corner with Uncle Wizard following. Suddenly Bob screamed to a halt and danced with joy.

'We've got it! We've got it!' he cried.

Uncle Wizard scratched his head. They were at a dead-end, but there was no sign of the A-Tree.

It had simply vanished.

'Where is it?'

Bob pointed and laughed. On the far wall of the dead-end, hidden by a deep, dark shadow was a garden shed stuck in the wall. It's door was slightly ajar.

'It has to be in there,' said Bob with glee.

Uncle Wizard and Bob tiptoed silently towards the shed. As they reached the door Uncle Wizard put a finger to his lips.

'Not a sound,' he whispered.

The shed was silent. Nothing stirred. Uncle Wizard reached out and grasped the handle. As his fingers gripped the metal firmly he turned to Bob.

'Ready, after three. 1...2...'

But Uncle Wizard never got to 3.

The doors of the shed burst open. Out leapt the A-Tree. But Bob was too quick. As the A-Tree sprinted for its life he snapped out his beak and plucked off a perfect A-Leaf from one of its branches.

'I got it, I got it,' he cried, 'triple pie for me!'

Bob danced about on his two tiny legs. He whooped and hollered and proudly displayed the A-Leaf. They had the second part of the Spell of Forever! But Uncle Wizard did not dance for joy. He had a look of utter horror on his face.

'I'm not sure that was such a good idea,' he said nervously.

Bob heard a noise from behind him. It was a deep, angry growl. He turned around and there, towering above him, was the A-Tree. It stared down at him with furious, raging eyes.

'Aah,' said Uncle Wizard.

'Oh dear,' said Bob.

The A-Tree took a giant stride towards them. They were engulfed by its huge shadow.

'Who dares snatch one of my leaves?' growled the A-Tree menacingly.

Uncle Wizard gulped. Bob gasped. The A-Tree took another stride towards them. They were trapped against the wall.

'Any ideas?' said Bob.

'Err…erm…err,' stuttered Uncle Wizard.

The A-Tree was on top of them. It growled hideously and raised a jagged, terrifying branch.

'No one steals my leaves!!!'

And just as the A-Tree was about to strike a washing machine said something rather peculiar.

'Well, well, well,' it exclaimed importantly, 'it's Uncle Wizard! Fancy seeing you here.'

Uncle Wizard's mouth fell open in astonishment.

'It can't be…'

# 28

Uncle Wizard gasped at the washing machine.

'What's going on?' asked Bob.

'You're not going to believe this,' said Uncle Wizard, 'but I know that washing machine.'

Bob shrugged.

'Well, we all have strange friends. Have I ever told you about Alan the Pigeon?'

'No, no, you don't understand…'

Just then the A-Tree let out a furious roar. Uncle Wizard and Bob ducked as its swishing branch sliced through the air just above their heads.

'…you don't understand,' gasped Uncle Wizard breathlessly, 'that washing machine is a wizard. It's Duke Wizard!'

The washing machine nodded.

'Yes, yes, it is I, Duke Wizard, the most handsome wizard with the most magnificent moustache in the whole of Wizard HQ.'

Bob looked rather puzzled.

'So why have you turned yourself into a washing machine? I know you wizards are a strange bunch, but a washing machine, that's really odd…'

Duke Wizard growled.

'Foolish pigeon. This was not my doing. I was kidnapped by Grim Wizard in my quarters at Enchantment castle. I was taken on a flying-bus to his evil lair. He turned me into a washing machine and trapped me in this wall.'

Uncle Wizard's eyes shot wide open. Suddenly he realised what was happening.

'All the wizards are trapped in the walls…'

'What!' exclaimed Duke Wizard, 'then who's going to rescue me? I can't be a washing machine for the rest of my life. What will happen to my beautiful moustache?'

'I will rescue you,' said Uncle Wizard.

Duke Wizard scoffed loudly.

'What, you?' he said with a mocking laugh. 'But you're the worst wizard in the world. You'll probably turn everyone into turnips…'

Bob stamped his foot.

'Well he's doing a lot better than you are, Mr Washing Machine Wizard. What are you good for…washing underpants?'

'Now listen here you fat pigeon…'

'Fat! Who are you calling fat? I may enjoy the odd pie, but fat! How dare you…'

As Duke Wizard and Bob argued, Uncle Wizard gasped for breath. All the Great Wizards had been kidnapped by Grim Wizard and trapped in the Maze of Infinity. All the wizards and all the people on the flying buses had been turned into objects to build the walls. The toasters, the chairs, everything, they were all people.

His head span. He tried to gather his thoughts. Trapped in the opposite wall was an enormous bouncy castle. It could only be Tubby Wizard, the fattest wizard in the whole of Wizard HQ.

'Bob, we have to stop Grim Wizard.'

'You're right about that,' agreed Bob nervously, 'but first we've got a slightly more urgent problem.'

Looming above them the A-Tree shook with rage. It stamped its trunk and howled into the bright morning sky.

'You stole one of my leaves. No one steals my leaves. I will tear you limb from limb…'

Uncle Wizard threw up his arms and groaned.

'I know,' he said apologetically, 'we should have asked and we're very sorry. My name is Uncle Wizard. I need one of your leaves for a spell.'

'What spell?' growled the A-Tree.

Uncle Wizard pulled out the scroll.

'The Spell of Forever. I'm here to save the World. I'm here to defeat Grim Wizard…'

The A-Tree's eyes widened like the brightest moon.

'The Spell of Forever! Why didn't you say. Grim Wizard must be stopped. The poor people trapped in the Maze of Infinity must be freed. Uncle Wizard, of course you may have one of my leaves.'

Uncle Wizard and Bob could barely believe their ears. They had the second part of the spell!

'Thank you!' cried Uncle Wizard.

Bob threw up his arms and Uncle Wizard jumped for joy. They leapt about the clearing with huge smiles on their faces. They really were going to save the world!

But so excited were they, neither of them thought to look at the scroll. Before, the third part of the Spell of Forever had read:

## TWI CHETH FO TRA HEETH

Now flashes of magic danced across the page. The scroll shimmered as the letters rearranged themselves. They shifted and shunted and then, in a twinkle of glittering light, the third part of the spell appeared. But it was too late. Uncle Wizard had already put the scroll back in his magic cloak.

It was a terrible mistake.

'So,' said Bob, 'how do we get out of here?'

Uncle Wizard shrugged and looked around. With all its twists and turns it could take them years to find their way out of the Maze of Infinity.

'I don't know, can anyone help us?'

He looked with hopeful eyes to the objects in the walls, but none of them would meet his gaze. Then he remembered the television that had suddenly exploded. Perhaps the objects were worried they too would be punished. With a deep breath and fire in his belly he stood on a boulder in the middle of the clearing.

'My name is Uncle Wizard and I need your help. I need to escape from the Maze of Infinity. With your help I can defeat Grim Wizard and save the World. You must show me the way out...'

There was a nervous silence. Uncle Wizard stared with desperate eyes, but the objects were too frightened to speak up.

Bob strode into the middle of the clearing.

'Come on, who's going to help Uncle Wizard? He's faced ghosts. He's faced Water Dragons and Thunder Trolls. He can defeat Grim Wizard. He can save the World. All he needs now is your help...'

Suddenly a milk bottle piped up.

'I'll help,' it cried out. 'Anything's better than being a milk bottle.'

There were gasps from around the walls, but bravely more and more volunteers came forward.

'I'll help,' said a lawn-mover.

'Me to,' said a wheelbarrow.

Soon a chorus echoed around the clearing. Help came in all shapes and sizes. Blankets, trumpets, book-cases and roller-skates, they all wanted to help Uncle Wizard.

And then the most amazing thing happened.

'Good grief!' exclaimed Uncle Wizard.

'Crumbs!' cried Bob.

The Maze of Infinity began to wriggle and stretch. The objects in the walls squeezed and squirmed, toasters against spades, post-boxes against clocks, until suddenly, with a great creaking sound, a hole appeared in the wall. Small at first, but quickly it began to grow.

Soon there was a tunnel right through the wall.

'Will you look at that!' said Bob in amazement.

Uncle Wizard peered through the hole. In the pathway beyond another hole was opening in the wall, and beyond that yet another. Every wall thrust and shunted to make a path to the exit of the Maze of Infinity.

Bob tugged at his bobble hat thoughtfully.

'How far do you think the exit is?'

'Hmm,' said Uncle Wizard, 'looks like a long way.'

The A-Tree coughed politely.

'Maybe I can be of assistance...'

Uncle Wizard and Bob suddenly found themselves plucked off the ground by the A-Tree. It spun them around in the air and placed them in a wheelbarrow which had become dislodged from the wall. The A-Tree took hold of the wheelbarrow's handles and faced the hole in the wall.

'Are you ready?'

Uncle Wizard and Bob nodded and the A-Tree was off. With huge, powerful strides it raced towards the first hole. With a bump the wheelbarrow bounced through the gap. Uncle Wizard and Bob had to cling on tight not to be thrown out. All the objects cheered as the wheelbarrow headed for the second hole.

With a bounce the wheelbarrow made it though the second hole and then picked up speed.

Quickly the Maze of Infinity became a blur. Uncle Wizard and Bob tried to wave to the objects, but their journey became a roller-coaster ride of flashing colours and babbling sound.

Up ahead the walls shifted and squirmed, each opening a path to the exit. The wheelbarrow was like an express train. The A-Tree gripped its handles as its thundering legs pounded across the floor. They hurtled through hole after hole. Uncle Wizard looked behind them for the centre of the maze, but that had long since disappeared.

For the rest of the morning they sped through the maze. Sometimes the A-Tree ducked left, sometimes it ducked right, but all the time the wheelbarrow clattered on towards the exit of the Maze of Infinity.

Eventually they began to slow down. The

maze became less of a blur, and Uncle Wizard and Bob could make out shapes and sounds far more clearly. With one final bump the wheelbarrow came to a halt.

'Well,' said the A-Tree, 'there's the exit...'

At the end of an overgrown pathway, covered with creepers, stood the exit of the Maze of Infinity. It looked so ordinary, for a moment Uncle Wizard and Bob just stared at it in disbelief.

The wheelbarrow coughed.

'I thought you had a world to save?'

'Yes, yes,' said Uncle Wizard as he and Bob climbed out of the wheelbarrow. 'Thank you for your help, and thank you Mr A-Tree for the leaf.'

The A-Tree smiled, said goodbye, and then with the wheelbarrow still held by its branches, disappeared back towards the centre of the maze.

'Well Bob, shall we make history?'

Bob stared at the exit archway.

'Let's do it.'

And with that they walked towards the exit of the Maze of Infinity. They brushed aside the creepers, ducked under the archway, and stepped out of the maze into the blazing sunshine. Above them a rusty counter wheezed and strained and then ticked over twice.

It now read:

*002*

First one person spotted them and then another. The sight of Uncle Wizard and Bob leaving the Maze of Infinity was incredible. There were cheers and claps and hearty slaps on the back. A huge crowd gathered, all wanting to hear their story.

When finally there was quiet Uncle Wizard told them all about the Maze of Infinity. The people were shocked. They could not believe it was being used by Grim Wizard. A thousand questions were shouted at once, but Uncle Wizard held up his hands for silence.

'Close the maze,' he cried. 'Close it now!'

The crowd quickly moved towards the entrance. Without another word the Maze of Infinity was boarded up.

Just then Bob spotted something in the sky. He tugged at Uncle Wizard's cloak.

'I think our ride has arrived.'

Out of the sky swooped The Witch's broomstick. In one swift movement it dived down and plucked Uncle Wizard and Bob off the ground. As they shot off into the sky Uncle Wizard looked back towards the Maze of Infinity. As soon as he had saved the World he had to return to free the people.

The broomstick zoomed through the sky.

'Where's it taking us?' asked Bob.

'To find the third part of the spell of course.'

'Which is what?'

Suddenly Uncle Wizard remembered the scroll. What was the final part of the spell? As the broomstick whooshed through the sky Uncle Wizard reached inside his cloak and pulled out the Spell of Forever. He unrolled it and began to read.

A look of horror appeared on his face.

'Oh, no!' he exclaimed in utter dismay. 'It can't

be, it can't be...'

'What is it?' asked Bob. 'What's the third part of the spell?'

Uncle Wizard shook his head.

'I can't do it, Bob. I can't save the World. Grim Wizard has won…'

# 29

Uncle Wizard quietly asked the broomstick to land. His face was pale and his eyes were sunken. The broomstick landed in a field and Uncle Wizard climbed off.

'Where are you going?' asked Bob.

Uncle Wizard just shrugged his shoulders and walked away from the broomstick with his head bowed low.

Bob did not know what to do. They had battled monsters and ghosts. They had escaped the Maze of Infinity, but now everything seemed lost. Uncle Wizard had given up. What was the third part of the spell? Why was it so impossible?

Bob shook his head. He watched Uncle Wizard disappear across the field. Their wonderful adventure seemed over.

'How could she do this to me?' said Uncle Wizard with his head in his hands.

Bob found Uncle Wizard sat by the edge of a huge waterfall throwing pebbles into the tumbling water.

'She knew what the third part of the spell was all along. She should have told me.'

Bob grimaced.

'What is the third part?' he asked quietly.

Uncle Wizard pulled out the scroll and stared at it in utter despair. A tear rolled down his cheek. Below *Tooth of a Thunder Troll*, below *An A-Leaf*, was written the final part of the spell. It said simply:

## *THE HEART OF THE WITCH*

Bob gasped.  He saw the pain written on Uncle Wizard's face.

'I can't take The Witch's heart,' he said.  'She will die.'

'Not even to save the world?' asked Bob.

'Not even for that,' said Uncle Wizard.

Uncle Wizard and Bob sat in silence as the day grew longer.  The only sound was the tumbling waterfall and the occasional twitter of a gloom-bird. Now and then Uncle Wizard would throw another pebble, but he did not care if it splashed into the water or landed with a splat on the muddy river-bank.

'There has to be another way,' said Bob eventually.

Uncle Wizard shook his head.

'I've sat here and I've thought and thought,' he said with the longest of sighs. 'There is no other way. To defeat Grim Wizard I need the heart of The Witch. I can't do that, I care so much about her.'

Suddenly Bob's eyes lit up.

'That's it!' he cried joyously.

'That's what?' said Uncle Wizard gloomily.

Bob was on his feet. He jumped up and down and shrieked in excitement.

'I've worked it out. I know how you can save the world!'

'How?' said Uncle Wizard hesitantly.

Bob laughed.

'Haven't you worked it out yet?'

Uncle Wizard shook his head. He was upset and was not in the mood for playing games. Bob smiled and danced over to Uncle Wizard. He jumped up and landed on his shoulder.

'I'll tell you then…'

He leant over and whispered into Uncle Wizard's ear. With a few simple words he explained just how he could defeat Grim Wizard. Uncle Wizard's eyes lit up. He could hardly believe what he heard.

'Surely not?' he exclaimed.

'Oh yes,' said Bob. 'Oh yes indeed!'

An enormous smile burst onto Uncle Wizard's face. There was still a chance he could save the World and save The Witch.

'What are we waiting for then! Come on…!'

Uncle Wizard leapt to his feet and raced across the field like lightning. Bob clung to his magic cloak as they hurtled through the grass back to the waiting broomstick. They leapt onboard and shot off into the sky.

'Back to Wizard HQ!' shouted Uncle Wizard with joy. 'Ride like the wind.'

The broomstick flew faster than it had ever flown before. It rocketed over The Lurking Jungle and blasted through Tumble Canyon. It buzzed the top of Mood Man Mountain and scattered a flock of sparkle-moths fluttering above a sun-tree.

The broomstick began to descend. It dived through the clouds and landed in a field.

'Well, here we are again, Bob.'

In the middle of the field stood a brilliant white door. The door that led back to Wizard HQ.

'Wow,' said Bob, 'seems like a long time since we were here.'

Uncle Wizard smiled.

'Certainly does.'

'So now what?'

Uncle Wizard thanked the broomstick and then faced the brilliant white door. He turned the handle and stepped back into Wizard HQ.

'Now we go and save the World...'

# 30

The brilliant white door closed with a creak. Uncle Wizard and Bob were back in Wizard HQ. They stood in the dark muddy passageway at the very bottom of Wizard HQ and stared into the darkness.

'Well, its nice to be back,' said Uncle Wizard.

Bob gasped. A terrible, biting coldness chilled Wizard HQ. Shadows flickered ominously.

'Are you mad? This place is probably crawling with Ghoths. Something's going to eat us for sure.'

Uncle Wizard shook his head defiantly.

'This isn't a day for getting eaten. This is a day for saving the world. Come on, this way!'

Uncle Wizard took a flaming torch from the wall and they set off along the passageway. The ground squelched and thick green slime covered the walls. With cautious steps they fumbled their way to the staircase at the end of the passageway. At the foot of the stairs they stopped and looked upwards. The staircase spiralled up into more murky darkness.

'Grim Wizard is up there, somewhere,' said Uncle Wizard.

'Do you think he knows we're here?'

A deep booming laugh shook Wizard HQ.

'I think we're expected…'

They crept up the stairs on tiptoes. Every time the staircase creaked, Bob flinched, certain something was going to eat him. By the time they reached the top Bob was sure he had seen ten Ghoths and a Mega-Demon hiding in the shadows.

'Which way now?'

They stood in the middle of a landing. Harris the Caretaker had led them through the corridors at such a speed that Uncle Wizard could not remember the way to The Great Hall.

'Erm, err, I think we should...'

Suddenly a floorboard creaked at the far end of the landing. Out of the darkness came a Ghoth on patrol.

Uncle Wizard gasped.

'Quick...hide!'

The Ghoth slithered and slurped across the landing. Its blood red eyes searched the darkness for the slightest movement.

'Over there...' whispered Bob.

On the opposite wall stood a statue of Hero Wizard. Uncle Wizard and Bob dashed across the landing and hid behind the statue. They dared not breathe. They dared not move.

The Ghoth approached. From the far end of the landing its maggoty legs carried its stinking body ever nearer. Suddenly the Ghoth stuck its bulbous nose in the air and sniffed. It had picked up a scent. Another sniff and it stopped in its tracks. Slowly, menacingly it turned towards the statue.

'You will surrender!' cried the Ghoth. 'You will be taken to our Master.'

Uncle Wizard gasped, they were certain to be captured. Desperately he tapped Bob on the shoulder. Bob looked up and Uncle Wizard motioned with his hand.  Bob nodded and quickly slipped into the shadows, away from the statue.

The Ghoth approached the statue.  Its stench was hideous.  Slime oozed from its mouth.

'Our Master will punish you.'

Uncle Wizard took a deep breath.  He had only one chance.  With a bellowing cry he leapt out from behind the statue and made a desperate bid to barge past the Ghoth.

With all his might he knocked the Ghoth flying. With a surge of hope he dashed into the murky darkness of the landing, only to run straight into a second Ghoth on patrol.  The Ghoth's huge powerful arms grabbed Uncle Wizard and wrestled him to the ground.  The other Ghoth quickly recovered and in a flash they had bound Uncle Wizard's hands with rope.

'Now you will face our Master.'

From the shadows of the wall Bob could only watch in horror as the Ghoths dragged Uncle Wizard off into the darkness.

Everything seemed lost.

# 31

'We're doomed!'

The landing fell silent as the two slavering Ghoths dragged Uncle Wizard into the darkness. What could Bob do now? There was no way he could defeat the Ghoths on his own.

'Come on Bob, think,' he said to himself, 'think like you've never thought before.'

Frantically he paced up and down. He had to do something or Grim Wizard had won.

'There must be a solution...there's always a solution...perhaps a solution involving pies...no, no, stop thinking about pies. Isn't there anyone who can help?'

Suddenly he had it.

'Yes! Harris the Caretaker,' he cried, 'he'll know what to do.'

Harris had said he could always be found in The Secret Library. There was only one problem...

'Where's The Secret Library?' said Bob to himself.

Bob looked up and down the landing. Wizard HQ was full of twists and turns. With no time to lose he chose a staircase on the opposite side of the landing, and waddled up it as fast as his legs would carry him.

He searched everywhere. He walked down corridor after corridor, peered in forgotten halls and silent kitchens, but there was no sign of The Secret Library.

'Come on, it has to be round here somewhere?'

'And what may that be?'

Bob jumped in fright. In the wall a wooden carving of an owl had come to life. It was a magnificent bird, its feathers ornate and regal.

'Erm, I'm looking for The Secret Library.'

'The Secret Library!' exclaimed the owl, 'my, my, my a pigeon who can read. Whatever next!'

Bob gritted his teeth.

'I need to find the library. Do you know where it is?' he asked urgently.

The owl ruffled its feathers.

'Do I, Barnard the Owl know where The Secret Library is? My, what an absurd question. I know everything. I am the wisest of the wise owls, wiser even than...*ouch!*'

Bob found a spell-book and threw it at Barnard the Owl. It hit him on the nose.

'Sorry, which way was that?'

Barnard the Owl cowered his head and pointed coyly towards a corridor.

'Just down there,' he mumbled.

'Thank you,' said Bob, 'pleasure doing business with you.'

Bob sped off down the corridor. He turned left, turned right and then suddenly his eyes lit up. There were the elegantly carved doors of The Secret Library. He cautiously approached the doors and then carefully nudged them open and slipped inside.

The Secret Library was eerily quiet. Shadows fell across the books and the floor creaked. With timid steps Bob crept into the darkness.

'If there are Ghoths in here, I'm done for,' he whispered to himself.

His head jerked nervously this way and that. His legs shook and his knees trembled. He crept slowly along an aisle of high towering bookcases. Every flicker of light, every speckle of dust made him jump.

'Ggggrraaaahhhh!!!'

Suddenly a shadow leapt out at him. A coarse, craggy hand grabbed him and stuffed him into a sack. He tried to struggle, tried to scream, but the sack was pulled tight and knotted.

'If I get a last request, can it be a pie?'

'Bob the Pigeon?'

The sack was untied in an instant. The same

coarse hand reached in and pulled him out. It belonged to Harris the Caretaker.

'Sorry Bob, I didn't realise it was you. There are Ghoths everywhere. Where's Uncle Wizard?'

Bob told him everything. How they had journeyed through the Land of Forever, battled the Water Dragon, defeated the Thunder Troll and escaped the Maze of Infinity. Now they had come back to Wizard HQ to defeat Grim Wizard, but Uncle Wizard had been captured.

'They'll be taking him to The Great Hall, that's where Grim Wizard is. I think we can get there before them.'

'How?' asked Bob.

Harris tapped his nose.

'No one knows Wizard HQ like I do.'

Bob groaned.

'It's going to be something terrifying isn't it?'

But before Bob could complain, Harris picked him up and raced across the library. In front of them was a huge painting of the Great Wizards looking resplendent in their finest Wizard Day robes. Harris flicked a switch and the painting shot up into the ceiling. Behind it was a hole in the wall.

'It's a lift,' said Harris. 'The wizards used it to bring books down to the library. I've modified it, a lot...'

Bob closed his eyes.

'I'm not going to enjoy this am I?'

Harris smiled.

'Have you ever been fired out of a cannon?'

Bob shook his head.

'Good, then you wont know how scared you should be.'

They clambered into the lift. It was cramped, but they managed to squeeze inside. Harris pressed a button and the doors slammed shut. For a moment the lift sat idle, then ominously it began to rumble. It shook, shuddered, then suddenly blasted off like a space rocket.

'Aaaaaaarrrrghhhhh!' screamed Bob.

The lift hurtled upwards at a frightening speed. It clanged and clattered against the lift-shaft and seemed as if it would shake to pieces at any second.

'Almost there,' shouted Harris above the deafening noise.

Bob shook like a leaf.

'We're doomed!'

Just then the clang and clatter began to lessen. The ride became smoother and much to Bob's relief the lift came to a halt.

'This is the ground floor,' said Harris as the lift doors opened. 'The Ghoths will bring Uncle Wizard this way. Here's the plan...'

# 32

A hideous snarl echoed through the corridors of Wizard HQ. The Ghoths slithered through the shadows and headed for The Great Hall. Between them, hands bound, was the only wizard who could save the World.

Uncle Wizard struggled again, but it was hopeless. Was this it? Had he failed? Soon he would be in the clutches of Grim Wizard and the World would be doomed.

'I'd stop right there if I were you.'

Suddenly, out of the shadows, stepped something small and pigeon-like. Heroically it stood in front of the Ghoths and blocked their path.

'Bob?' exclaimed Uncle Wizard in surprise.

'Don't take another step,' said Bob dramatically.

Uncle Wizard looked aghast.

'Run Bob, run,' he cried, 'it's hopeless.'

Bob casually leaned against a pillar and pulled out a splendid looking pie. He took a bite and chewed thoughtfully before pointing at Uncle Wizard.

'That there is my friend,' said Bob through mouthfuls of pie. 'No one captures my friend and gets away with it.'

'Bob, what's got into you?' cried Uncle Wizard. 'The Ghoths will eat you alive!'

Bob shook his head and took another bite of pie.

'Someone told me that this isn't a day for getting eaten. This is a day for saving the World. Plus you're forgetting something…'

Uncle Wizard looked utterly bewildered.

'And that is?'

Bob smiled.

'Never underestimate the power of the frying-pan.'

'What…?'

The Ghoths growled and stared at Bob with vicious eyes. They bared their teeth, sharpened their claws and were just about to attack, when:

*Clang!*

Out of the shadows swung a frying-pan and whacked one of the Ghoths over the head. For a moment the Ghoth looked utterly astonished before it staggered about, and then toppled to the floor with a crunching thud. In a flash the frying-pan swung again.

*Clang!*

The second Ghoth crumpled to the floor and then Harris the Caretaker stepped out of the shadows.

'Good frying-pan work,' said Bob.

'Thank you,' said Harris with a nod.

Quickly they untied Uncle Wizard. He rubbed his wrists and thanked his rescuers.

Harris looked around.

'You haven't got much time, more Ghoths will be along soon.'

But there was only one thing on Uncle Wizard's mind.

'Have you seen The Witch?'

Harris took a deep breath.

'Grim Wizard brought her to Wizard HQ. She looked…lifeless.'

The corridor fell silent. Uncle Wizard stared at the floor in utter dismay. He took deep breaths and puffed out his cheeks. Eventually he looked up.

'She's all right,' he said purposefully.

'How do you know?' asked Bob.

Uncle Wizard paused for a moment.

'Because she has to be, that's all. Now come on, we have a world to save.'

Harris pointed towards the end of the corridor.

'The Great Hall is down there. That's where you'll find Grim Wizard. Now, if you'll excuse me, I have work to do. There are more Ghoths to round up.'

Harris scooped the two groaning Ghoths into a sack and dragged them away.

'Good luck,' he said as he disappeared into the darkness.

Uncle Wizard and Bob watched him go, and then walked towards the magnificent doors of The Great Hall.

'Thank you for rescuing me,' said Uncle Wizard, 'and thank you for coming with me to the Land of Forever. I wouldn't have made it without you.'

Bob smiled.

'We can talk about my reward later.'

'Will it be a reward of pies?'

'Hmm,' said Bob nodding, 'now there's an idea.'

Uncle Wizard smiled and then composed himself. Beyond the doors of The Great Hall the most evil wizard to ever live was waiting for them.

Bob tugged at his bobble hat nervously.

'You do know what you're doing, don't you?'

Uncle Wizard smiled.

'I'm Uncle Wizard. Of course I know what I'm doing.'

And with that Uncle Wizard pushed open the doors to The Great Hall and came face to face with Grim Wizard.

# 33

The door closed with the quietest of clicks. Uncle Wizard and Bob walked into The Great Hall and turned to face the throne.

'SO, PATHETIC WIZARD ARRIVES AT LAST.'

There sat Grim Wizard, the most evil wizard to ever live. His long, spindly fingers twitched like the legs of a ravenous spider. His dark red eyes glowed with the fire of a mighty volcano. Around him, the air was mangled by the aura of his evil magic.

Uncle Wizard stared at Grim Wizard. He took a deep breath and cleared his throat.

'My name is Uncle Wizard.'

Grim Wizard laughed. It was a sound more gruesome than the cries of terror from the deepest darkest dungeon. Bob shuddered but Uncle Wizard stood tall and proud. He even took a step forwards.

'I am here to save the world.'

'YOU WILL FAIL.'

Grim Wizard rose from the throne. He towered high above Uncle Wizard and cast his arms out across The Great Hall.

'SEE THE GREAT WIZARDS…'

Uncle Wizard turned around. The walls of The Great Hall were lined with paintings of the Great Wizards. There was Lord Wizard, his flowing beard white and gleaming. There was Major Wizard, his medals shining brightly. On and on they went;

Captain Wizard, Gruff Wizard and Danger Wizard.

'...I DEFEATED THEM ALL. THEY ALL SURRENDERED TO MY POWER. AND YES...'

A mocking snarl appeared on the face of Grim Wizard. His voice was cold and callous.

'...I ALSO DEFEATED THE WITCH.'

Grim Wizard clicked his fingers. High up in the ceiling of The Great Hall a sheet fluttered to the wooden floor. It revealed a cage. Trapped in the cage was The Witch.

Uncle Wizard gasped. The cage swung high above the floor and was surrounded by spitting, hissing devil-light.

'SHE IS TRAPPED BY MY MAGIC. SHE CAN NEVER ESCAPE.'

Uncle Wizard looked up. The Witch was shackled by chains. Her body was slumped and unconscious.

'HOW WILL YOU DEFEAT ME NOW? THE SPELL OF FOREVER IS USELESS WITHOUT THE HEART OF THE WITCH.'

Suddenly Uncle Wizard felt very small. He was dwarfed by The Great Hall, and dwarfed by the power of Grim Wizard. A cold shiver rippled through his body. He turned to the light streaming through the giant window at the far end of The Great Hall, but even that did not warm him. He felt lost. The plan seemed so simple when Bob had whispered it to him at the waterfall. Now, stood before Grim Wizard, everything looked hopeless.

Bob looked at Uncle Wizard and shook his head.

'Well, I'm not putting up with this. I want my reward of pies...'

He took a bold step forwards.

'Now listen here, Mr Grim Wizard. I'm getting a little annoyed with you. I could quite happily be sitting in our wigwam eating pie, but, oh no, you had to come stomping in here taking over the World. Well, I for one have had enough. Uncle Wizard is going to defeat you, and how do I know he's going to defeat you, well...'

Uncle Wizard gulped.

'Erm, Bob, I'm not sure this is helping...'

Grim Wizard let out a deafening roar. His shadow filled the Great Hall and his eyes glowed with raging fire.

'I GROW BORED OF THESE GAMES.'

Suddenly a huge urn hurled itself across The Great Hall, straight at Uncle Wizard and Bob. They just managed to dive for cover as the urn smashed into the wooden floor.

'THE GREAT WIZARDS TRIED TO IMPRISON ME FOR ALL ETERNITY. THEY FAILED. I NOW RULE THE WORLD.'

Grim Wizard took a menacing step forwards.

'AND NOW PATHETIC WIZARD, YOU WILL PAY FOR YOUR FOOLISHNESS.'

Vicious devil-light ripped out of Grim Wizard's fingers. It shot like a sizzling bolt of lightning through The Great Hall and slammed straight into Uncle Wizard. He tumbled to the ground, winded and gasping.

A cruel laugh echoed through the hall.

'ALL THE GREAT WIZARDS FELL AT MY FEET. ALL SURRENDED TO GRIM WIZARD...'

Uncle Wizard coughed and spluttered. He had never felt pain like this before. His body felt as if it had been dragged over rocks and boulders.

'...NOW YOU SHALL SUFFER THEIR FATE AND THE WHOLE WORLD WILL KNOW, I AM INVINCIBLE.'

Suddenly it was real. Uncle Wizard understood the true power of Grim Wizard. The Great Wizards had been defeated, and just a single blast of devil-light had him crying out in agony. He could not do this alone.  In desperation he called out to The Witch.

'Please, I need your help.'

The Witch lay slumped in the cage.  Her body was crooked and her eyes were glazed.  Evil magic crackled about her.

Uncle Wizard cried out again.

'You must hear me.  Please.  I need your help.'

Grim Wizard laughed, but Uncle Wizard ignored him.  With pleading eyes he stared at the cage, at The Witch's face, the most beautiful face he had ever seen.

And then it happened.

It was not just a flicker of light, not just a shadow, The Witch had smiled, he was sure of it.  He felt elated.  The pain evaporated from his body.  He could do it.  He could save the World.  Uncle Wizard stood up.  He brushed himself down and stared squarely into the eyes of Grim Wizard.

'No one is invincible.  I will defeat you.'

A heart-stopping silence gripped The Great Hall.  Through the paintings the eyes of the Great Wizards seemed to look upon Uncle Wizard with growing hope.

'I travelled through the Land of Forever.  I defeated the Thunder Troll.  I beat the Maze of Infinity...'

Uncle Wizard took a brave step forwards.  He felt in his pocket for the Tooth of the Thunder Troll and the A-Leaf.  They gave him strength.

'...and now Grim Wizard, I will defeat you.'

Grim Wizard stared into the eyes of Uncle

Wizard.  He spoke only one word.

'FOOL.'

A deathly light rippled on his fingers.  It rasped and raged, straining to be free.  Suddenly Grim Wizard threw out his hands and unleashed a bolt of the most grotesque devil-light at Uncle Wizard.

The Great Hall seemed to explode.  The devil-light slammed into Uncle Wizard and hurled him through the air like a rag doll.

Bob could only watch in horror as Uncle Wizard smashed sickeningly through the huge glass window at the end of The Great Hall.  The glass fell to the floor in tiny shattered pieces.  A terrible silence followed.

Bob felt numb.  His head buzzed.  For a moment he could not move.  He stared in shock at the shattered window.

And then Bob screamed.

In a flash he raced across The Great Hall and leapt through the shattered window.

Uncle Wizard lay in the middle of Wizard Street in a terrible tangle of arms and legs.

He was not moving…

# 34

A cold wind blew through Wizard Street. Rain fell silently. Uncle Wizard lay in the middle of the road, his hat crooked, and his cloak mangled. Bob gasped. He looked more like a heap of dirty old clothes than the only wizard to beat the Maze of Infinity.

'Can you hear me?' asked Bob softly.

Uncle Wizard did not answer. His face was grazed and his body battered. A drop of rain fell into his eye and dribbled down his cheek. It was as if Uncle Wizard was crying, but still he did not move.

'Uncle Wizard, can you hear me?'

Bob lowered his head. Everything had gone wrong. The Witch had been captured and Uncle Wizard lay lifeless. From inside Wizard HQ came the most callous, evil laugh that Bob had ever heard. It stabbed at his heart.

'This can't be happening.'

A rumble of thunder boomed across the sky and lightning flashed. Bob stood alone; cold, wet and with a feeling of utter despair.

'It wasn't meant to be like this,' he said sadly, 'no one was meant to get hurt. We were going to save the World and then go back to the wigwam for a cup of tea and a piece of pie. Now look at you, all broken and bruised. It's not fair. It's just not fair.'

Bob stared at the darkening clouds.

'We've come all this way. We've done so many things. We slid down the river of ice, we caught a lift with a waddling-rock, and we scared the ghosts of Haunted Hill, and it was all for nothing. And what about The Witch? Remember what I said to you at the waterfall. She loves you...'

Bob shook his head and turned back to Uncle Wizard.

'...and I know you love her and she's trapped in there with Grim Wizard and unless you wake up, unless you get up and go and save her, everything is doomed...'

The rain fell and the wind howled.

'Come on Uncle Wizard!' cried Bob, 'Get up!'

Wizard Street paused for a breathless second. A flash of lightning lit up the sky. Suddenly one of Uncle Wizard's eyes popped open.

'Uncle Wizard!' exclaimed Bob.

Uncle Wizard groaned.

'Bob?' he said groggily.

'Yes, yes!' cried Bob, 'that's me! Bob the Pigeon, tubby, likes a pie or two.'

'Bob, Bob,' wheezed Uncle Wizard, 'The Witch...'

'Yes?'

'...she, she smiled at me.'

Suddenly Uncle Wizard leapt to his feet. He winced and then swayed about as if he were a scarecrow in a thunderstorm.

'Bob, I feel rather peculiar.'

'Erm, that's a lamppost you're talking to,' said Bob, 'I'm over here.'

Uncle Wizard spun round.

'Oh yes, excellent. Now, I've got something terribly important to do, what is it, what is it?'

Uncle Wizard scratched his head and looked thoughtful.

Bob coughed politely.

'Erm, you've got to save the World.'

Uncle Wizard clicked his fingers.

'That's it! That's the fellow. Save the World. I knew it was something important. Come on, this way!'

Bob looked concerned.

'You do know what you're doing, don't you?'

A huge grin appeared on Uncle Wizard's face.

'Bob, this may come as a surprise to you, but I have absolutely no idea what I'm doing...'

'What?'

'...and that is why I shall win. That is why I'll defeat Grim Wizard.'

Uncle Wizard dusted himself down, checked

his hat and cloak, and then leapt back through the huge smashed window of Wizard HQ.

'FOOL. YOU SHOULD HAVE FLED.'

Uncle Wizard stood in front of the window. The wind ruffled his clothes and a crash of lightning cast a golden aura around his body. He looked up at Grim Wizard.

'My name is Uncle Wizard. I am here to save the World.'

Grim Wizard howled with laughter.

'I AM GRIM WIZARD. THE MOST EVIL WIZARD TO EVER LIVE. I NOW RULE THE WORLD. I AM INVINCIBLE. NOT EVEN THE ANCIENT SPELLS OF THE GREAT WIZARDS CAN HARM ME.'

Uncle Wizard shrugged.

'Probably not, but I think you're forgetting something. I'm not a Great Wizard and I don't know any ancient spells.'

Grim Wizard growled.

'PATHETIC WIZARD. I CAN DEFEAT ANY SPELL KNOWN TO WIZARDS. HOW CAN YOU POSSIBLY DEFEAT ME?'

Uncle Wizard looked up at Grim Wizard.

'Because,' he said with a smile, 'I don't know what I'm doing…'

Just for a moment Grim Wizard looked puzzled.

'And,' continued Uncle Wizard, 'if I don't know what I'm doing, how can you possibly know?'

Grim Wizard flinched.

'Here Bob, hold this open for me.'

Uncle Wizard passed his magic hat to Bob and strode towards Grim Wizard.

'You might be able to defeat any spell known to wizards, but who knows what this spell will be? It could be anything.'

Uncle Wizard's hands dived into his pockets. He pulled out random potions and any old powder and threw them into his wizards hat. The hat began to froth and bubble with the most alarming colours.

Grim Wizard roared with fury.

'YOU ARE A FOOLISH WIZARD. YOU WILL BE DESTROYED.'

His fingers crackled with spitting magic. He threw up his hands and blasted a vicious thunder-bolt straight at Uncle Wizard.

This time Uncle Wizard was ready. In one smooth movement he did a forward roll, ducked under the thunder-bolt, and leapt back to his feet.

'My turn now.'

Uncle Wizard's hat burst with magic. There was a cascade of colours. Sparkling, fizzing light exploded in the air. Uncle Wizard poured in a whole bottle of whiz-bang powder and the spell screamed with wondrous energy.

From out of the magic hat rose a glowing ball of pure white light. It sparkled serenely in the dusky light of The Great Hall. Grim Wizard stared at it uneasily. His fingers still sizzled with devil-light. He lifted his hands, ready to strike, but it was too late. The gleaming ball of white light shot across The Great Hall. It hit him squarely in the chest.

The Great Hall exploded with colour. Grim

Wizard screamed. In one sudden movement he was flung backwards and pinned to the throne. He could not move.

'Not so invincible now,' said Bob.

Suddenly there was a monstrous cracking sound from above. Grim Wizard's spell was broken. The cage in which The Witch was trapped was disintegrating. In one final flash of light the cage vanished and The Witch plummeted downwards. Uncle Wizard steadied himself, moved this way and that, and then caught her perfectly in his arms.

'Why thank you kind wizard,' said The Witch with a smile.

Uncle Wizard just stared into The Witch's eyes with a silly grin on his face.

'Err, excuse me,' said Bob. 'I don't mean to interrupt or anything, but haven't you got one last spell to do?'

Uncle Wizard coughed.

'Err, yes, sorry, be right with you.'

Uncle Wizard gently put The Witch on the floor and then faced Grim Wizard. From his cloak he pulled out the tooth of the Thunder Troll and the A-Leaf. He held them in his hands and looked into Grim Wizard's eyes.

'My name is Uncle Wizard. I am going to save the World.'

Grim Wizard's face boiled with anger. He stared back at Uncle Wizard and a strained laugh struggled its way out of his mouth.

'PATHETIC WIZARD. YOU ONLY HAVE TWO PARTS OF THE SPELL. YOU STILL NEED

THE HEART OF THE WITCH.'

The Witch smiled.

'Oh, I think he already has that.'

And with that she leaned over to Uncle Wizard and gently kissed him.

Uncle Wizard threw up his arms and a rainbow of twinkling magic danced out of his hands. It arced gracefully through the air and engulfed Grim Wizard.

Grim Wizard never had time to scream. He simply disappeared in a flash of swirling light.

Uncle Wizard had won. He had defeated Grim Wizard. He had saved the World.

# 35

'Move along there, no dawdling.'

The twin suns of the Land of Forever blazed brightly. The occasional cloud dotted the sky and a soothing wind gently gusted by.

'Teapots to the right…if you were a teapot, please move to the right. Dustbins to the left…'

Grim Wizard's spell had been broken. The towering walls of the Maze of Infinity had turned back into people. Everyone who had been a television, an ironing board, a bean bag, anything; they were all free. One by one they staggered out of the exit.

'Don't worry, we'll get you all home soon…'

Uncle Wizard, Bob and The Witch had returned to the Land of Forever after Grim Wizard had been defeated. First they made sure the river of ice was running freely, and then went straight to the Maze of Infinity. As the people left the maze Bob marked them off on a clipboard.

'This is the last call for egg-cups. If you were an egg-cup can you quickly make your way to gate 43 where your flying-cow is waiting to depart.'

With bleary eyes and tired limbs the people climbed onboard their flying-cow. As one took off, another landed. The sky was full of a thousand flying cows, each one soaring off in a different direction.

'This will take forever, won't it?' said Uncle Wizard. 'There are thousands of people.'

The Witch smiled.

'We'll get them all home, won't we boys?'

Lance and Stallion the Flying Cows shrieked in dismay and covered their eyes.

'Don't talk to us!' cried Lance.

'And don't look at us either,' pleaded Stallion. 'We have work to do, and it wont help if you turn us to stone...'

With their heads bowed Lance and Stallion flew off into the bright blue sky, carrying a group of rather dazed and confused people back home.

The day drew on and still the people struggled out of the maze. The flying-cows worked double shifts, and were relieved when help came from a flock of aero-camels and hover-pigs. Slowly, as the twin suns of the Land of Forever slipped towards the horizon the stream of people leaving the maze dried to a trickle. The sky began to clear and very soon only Uncle Wizard, Bob and The Witch stood outside the Maze of Infinity.

'Well, that must be everyone,' said Uncle Wizard.

The Witch smiled.

'Not quite everyone...'

Suddenly there came a great roar of excitement from the exit of the maze. Uncle Wizard turned around and his mouth fell open.

'There he is!'

Out of the exit strode every wizard in the World. All the Great Wizards, all the wizards that Grim Wizard had captured at Enchantment Castle. They were the last to leave the Maze of Infinity and as one they rushed towards Uncle Wizard.

'Stupendous!' cried Lord Wizard.

'Fantastic!' yelled Hero Wizard.

'Wonderful!' chorused the rest.

Before he knew it Uncle Wizard had been hoisted onto the shoulders of the wizards. He was paraded around like a king. There were cheers, applause and cries of joy.

'Well, well, well,' said Lord Wizard proudly. 'Who'd have thought it! Uncle Wizard saving the World. Come, we must return to Wizard HQ. This is cause for a great celebration!'

Lord Wizard clicked his fingers and in a flash of magic, a flying carpet appeared.

'Hop on,' said Lord Wizard. 'You deserve to return to Wizard HQ in style!'

Uncle Wizard gasped. Only the most important wizards ever got to travel on Lord Wizard's flying carpet. Quickly he and Bob jumped on board.

'Aren't you coming with us?'

Uncle Wizard turned to The Witch. She remained on the ground, alone by the exit to the maze. Very slowly she shook her head.

'The Land of Forever is my home, Uncle Wizard. Grim Wizard did some terrible things to the people here. They need me...'

Uncle Wizard's heart sank.

'Will I ever see you again?'

But before The Witch could answer Lord Wizard clapped his hands and the magic carpet leapt into the air. The ground spiralled away and they soared into the dark night sky. Uncle Wizard looked back desperately, but there was nothing to see.

The ground was empty.

The Witch had gone.

# 36

Uncle Wizard sat in his wigwam sipping a cup of tea. Bob was on his perch nibbling a pie and flicking through a magazine. Outside the sun shone and the Happy Apples of Happy Apple Lane chatted to anyone who happened to pass by.

'So then what did you do?' asked Ellie.

'Well,' said Uncle Wizard, 'it was like this…'

It had been two weeks since Uncle Wizard had defeated Grim Wizard. He had been interviewed by reporters and had his picture in every newspaper. Only in the last few days had his life returned to normal and he was able to tell the children of Happy Apple Lane all about his adventure.

'…a giant Water Dragon burst out of the lake, shooting balls of flame from its nostrils…'

Uncle Wizard told Ellie, Joshua, Millie and Isabelle about Haunted Hill and the Thunder Troll. About the Maze of Infinity and his battle with Grim Wizard, but all they wanted to hear about was The Witch.

'Where is she now?' asked Ellie.

Bob the Pigeon looked up from his magazine. Uncle Wizard sighed.

'She needed to help the people of the Land of Forever. I haven't heard from her since. She didn't even come to the ceremony…'

Uncle Wizard had been presented with a Wizard Award for Excellent Services To Wizarding. It was a wonderful day, but without The Witch there, something was missing.

Just then there was a knock at the door of the wigwam. Uncle Wizard sighed.

'Probably another magazine wanting to do an interview, which one will it be this time?'

'Well,' said Bob holding up *Yoghurt World*, 'lets hope it's more exciting than this one.'

He began to read from the magazine:

*"Uncle Wizard, you defeated the Thunder Troll, beat the Maze of Infinity and saved the World, but what our readers really want to know is, black cherry or raspberry, what's your favourite flavour of yoghurt?"*

Uncle Wizard sighed.

'Perhaps I shouldn't answer it.'

'I rather hope you might,' said the voice from the other side of the door.

Uncle Wizard's eyes lit up. He rushed over to the door, pulled it open and there was The Witch. She looked even more beautiful than Uncle Wizard ever remembered.

'Good day fine wizard,' she said with a curtsey.

Uncle Wizard smiled.

'Good day Madam Witch,' he said with bow.

'Well, aren't you going to invite me in then?'

Uncle Wizard looked flustered for a moment.

'Yes, yes, please, come in, come in. Would you like a cup of tea?'

'That would be very nice,' said The Witch.

Uncle Wizard went to make the tea. The Witch said hello to Bob and then sat down on the sofa next to Ellie.

'Hello,' she said, 'what's your name?'

'I'm Ellie,' said Ellie, who then paused and thought for a moment. 'What's your name?'

'My name?' said The Witch with a chuckle. 'Oh, I don't have a name, I'm just called The Witch.'

'You've got to have a name,' said Ellie, 'everyone's got a name.'

'Oh right,' said The Witch, 'what do you think a good name for me would be, then?'

Ellie thought for a moment and then her eyes lit up.

'How about Auntie Witch?'

The Witch laughed.

'We'll see, we'll see.'

'What are you two giggling about?' said Uncle Wizard as he brought a steaming pot of tea over on a tray.

'Oh, nothing,' said The Witch, 'nothing at all.'

*The end*

*Coming Soon...*

The second book in the Uncle Wizard series:

# Uncle Wizard and the Golden Orb

The Wizard Day celebrations are approaching, but all is not well at Wizard HQ.  A series of strange goings-on have troubled the Wizard Council.  Even Lord Wizard is anxious…

Join Uncle Wizard and Bob the Pigeon as they set off on an epic adventure to find the Golden Orb…

For more information, and to read a sample of **Uncle Wizard and the Golden Orb** go to:

# www.unclewizard.co.uk

**Rules Review Publishing Ltd**
**London**